"Try not to overthink this, Ettore. You're of the age when you could reasonably be considering marriage. You're a good-looking young man from a good family. Finding a wife is hardly going to be a problem."

Wife. His fingertips bit into the fine porcelain. Even just hearing the word made his entire body tense. As the least favoured child in his family, he had trained himself not to rise, never to reveal emotion.

But that was before he met Dulcie.

With her messy blond hair and those blue eyes that made him feel like he was drowning and skydiving all at once. She was intoxicating. And he had been intoxicated. Which frankly was the only reasonable explanation for what he did.

For a moment, he pictured the fierce light in her eyes as she'd chosen her brother over him. Then he pushed the image away.

What he needed was a wife. A wife who would be willing to stand by his side and share his life and all its accompanying privileges and burdens.

What he wanted was a wife who would put him first above all others.

In other words, not Dulcie Turner.

Louise Fuller was a tomboy who hated pink and always wanted to be the prince—not the princess! Now she enjoys creating heroines who aren't pretty pushovers but are strong, believable women. Before writing for Harlequin, she studied literature and philosophy at university, then worked as a reporter on her local newspaper. She lives in Royal Tunbridge Wells with her impossibly handsome husband, Patrick, and their six children.

Books by Louise Fuller

Harlequin Presents

Returning for His Ruthless Revenge
Her Diamond Deal with the CEO
Royal Ring of Revenge
Business Between Enemies
Billion-Dollar Baby Clause

Hot Winter Escapes

One Forbidden Night in Paradise

Behind the Billionaire's Doors...

Undone in the Billionaire's Castle

The Diamond Club

Reclaimed with a Ring

Ruthless Rivals

Boss's Plus-One Demand
Nine-Month Contract

Visit the Author Profile page
at Harlequin.com for more titles.

MARCHESI'S MARRIAGE MANDATE

LOUISE FULLER

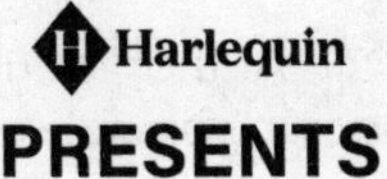

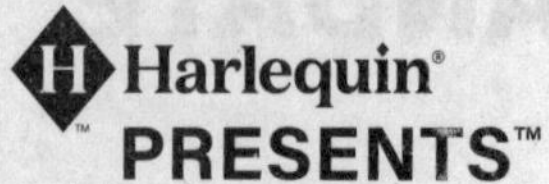

Recycling programs for this product may not exist in your area.

ISBN-13: 978-1-335-21387-7

Marchesi's Marriage Mandate

For questions and comments about the quality of this book, please contact us at CustomerService@Harlequin.com.

TM and ® are trademarks of Harlequin Enterprises ULC.

Harlequin Enterprises ULC
22 Adelaide St. West, 41st Floor
Toronto, Ontario M5H 4E3, Canada
www.Harlequin.com

HarperCollins Publishers
Macken House, 39/40 Mayor Street Upper,
Dublin 1, D01 C9W8, Ireland
www.HarperCollins.com

Printed in Lithuania

MARCHESI'S MARRIAGE MANDATE

PROLOGUE

The Marchesi apartment, Parioli district, Rome

'I FORGET, it's two sugars, isn't it?' Ettore Marchesi glanced at his lawyer, Carlo Biondi. He could have asked Mariana to stay and serve the coffee, but sometimes he liked to pretend that he was someone else. Someone other than the heir to the largest private estate in Italy.

There were other, older families. There were wealthier ones. Largely because his father and the rest of his freeloading relations preferred to tap into the Marchesi wealth to cover their expenses rather than work for a living.

Even his younger sister, Sofia, was happy to spend the family money. She had moved out of the Castiglione Fiana ten months ago, citing her need for freedom and independence, and was currently moving around the globe on the pretext of finding herself. But apparently freedom and independence didn't prevent her from using her title when it suited her to do so. And of course, his father, Edoardo, the current Duke of Marchesi, was still paying her bills.

His father.

Ettore rubbed the back of his neck, pushing against the knot of tension that had been there since Edoardo had been rushed into hospital two days ago.

Carlo cleared his throat. 'So how is he?'

Ettore met his gaze. Carlo was not just the Marchesi's' *avvocato*, he was one of the few people Ettore trusted with delicate family matters. Which was fortunate because his family were experts at creating chaos and drama.

'Mariana found him on the floor. She said he was barely breathing. But when I saw him earlier, he was playing *briscola* with the nurses.'

The old man was due to be discharged today. He would then have to wait until the doctor agreed that he was fit to fly back to Puglia.

The tension in Ettore's spine felt as if he were being racked. Edoardo wasn't even supposed to be in Rome. But Ettore's father was as incorrigible as he was stubborn. Being told that he couldn't do something simply intensified his desire to do so.

It was the story of Edoardo's life. Only this time his body had protested. He had collapsed, thankfully at the Marchesi apartment, and been taken to hospital. Bed rest and medication had stabilised his condition, but he was an eighty-six-year-old man, and his heart was failing.

'Have you called the family?'

Ettore shook his head. 'He wouldn't let me. And it's probably for the best. I don't need them roaring up in their supercars.'

'Will anything be leaked?' Carlo said softly.

Ettore shook his head again. 'I've dealt with the hospital before. They've always been very discreet.'

'That's good. We don't want any silly stories about the family curse doing the rounds.'

They did not.

Throughout history, many great dynasties had been

rumoured to have a curse on them. The Kennedys. The Grimaldis. In Italy it was the Marchesi family who had been troubled by unhappy marriages and untimely deaths across the generations.

His thumb moved to the now near invisible scar on his left wrist. There was another on his right shin and others on his stomach and back. Mementos of the bike crash that had killed Edo.

Despite their differences, he had loved his brother and still missed him. Sometimes he even missed his mother. Although she had made no secret of her preference for Edo. His father had been no less partisan in favouring Sofia, but he had never blamed him for the accident.

It was Edo's death that had elevated Ettore to the status of heir apparent. But he had been reluctantly managing his errant family since his grandfather died nearly twelve years ago.

Circling back to his original question, he lifted up the delicate porcelain sugar bowl.

'Not for me, sadly.' Carlo grimaced. 'I'm pre-diabetic and Carolina and Silvia are being very strict. One I could resist, but…' Carlo Biondi sighed, his face settling into an expression of resignation at the powerlessness of a man confronted by the combined willpower of his wife and daughter.

'And they're right. I know they are. Just because we want something doesn't mean we should allow ourselves to indulge our desires.'

Their eyes met briefly.

There was no need for either man to remark on the fact that indulging his desires was something Edoardo Marchesi did so often, it could have been the family's motto.

It wasn't.

The Marchesi motto was, somewhat laughably, *Guisto e Fidele*. Fair and faithful.

A commendable aim and no doubt, in the fragmented geopolitical landscape of what would one day become Italy, the first Duca Marchesi had been eagerly and honestly pledging his allegiance to his prince. Perhaps he was also faithful to his wife. But Ettore's forebears were notorious philanderers and unreliable in thought and word and deed.

For a moment, both men sipped their coffee in silence and then Carlo Biondi cleared his throat. 'But enough about my health. It's your father's I came to talk about.'

'You know as much as I do, Carlo. He's incredibly secretive about his medical history. He's over the worst. Probably if he follows the doctor's orders, he'll outlast us all.'

Carlo smiled stiffly. 'I know you want to believe that, Ettore, but we both know that your father is living on borrowed time.'

Some might say his interest repayments were long overdue, given his fondness for fine wine and beautiful, younger women.

'Which is why,' the lawyer continued seamlessly, 'it's time to discuss the will.'

'Has something changed?'

'No. The estate in its entirety passes to the oldest living heir.' The *avvocato* met his gaze. 'Since your brother's death, that is you. But you will have to satisfy the Corti-Marchesi clause.'

Ettore blinked. 'The Corti-Marchesi clause?' The

phrase was unfamiliar. Why, then, did it make a shiver of apprehension skim over his skin?

Carlo had finished his coffee.

'The clause is unswervable. It is enshrined in family tradition, but more importantly in law since the fifth duke decided that the responsibility of the estate was better suited to a married man.'

Married?

'The wording is archaic, but, in modern language, to inherit the estate, and its associated title, you must be married before the death of the current duke.'

'That's barbaric. No court would uphold such a clause.'

Carlo shrugged. 'I can assure you it's legally watertight. Challenging it in court would be a time-consuming, attention-drawing act that would fail, I'm sure.'

'And if I'm not married?'

The question hovered in the suddenly taut air between the two men.

'Then it will become necessary to share the clause with the rest of the family at the reading of the will.'

In other words, his right to inherit would be open to his uncle.

The thought appalled him. He loved his uncle, but Frederico was idle and irresponsible and fiscally incompetent. Surely this had to be a joke. But Carlo wasn't smiling. In fact, he had never looked more serious.

'Why have I never heard of this clause before?'

Carlo shrugged. 'Because it's never been an issue before. Previous heirs have always been married prior to the incumbent duke's death. Like your father. From memory, I'm not sure I even discussed the clause with him.'

Was that why Edoardo hadn't said anything to him?

Or was it because, for his father, Ettore was a useful tool. But not the child he would have picked to be his heir.

'Try not to overthink this, Ettore. You're of the age when you could reasonably be considering marriage. You're a good-looking young man from a good family. Finding a wife is hardly going to be a problem.'

Wife. His fingertips bit into the fine porcelain. Even just hearing the word made his entire body tense. As the least-favoured child in his family, he had trained himself not to rise, never to reveal emotion.

But that was before he met Dulcie.

With her soft, muddled blonde hair and those blue eyes that made him feel as though he were drowning and sky-diving all at once. She was intoxicating. And he had been intoxicated. Which frankly was the only reasonable explanation for what he had done.

For a moment, he pictured the fierce light in her eyes as she'd chosen her brother over him. Then he pushed the image away.

What he needed was a wife. A wife who would be willing to stand by his side and share his life and all its accompanying privileges and burdens.

What he wanted was a wife who would put him first above all others.

In other words, not Dulcie Turner.

Which meant finding a wife would have to wait.

First off, he needed to get a divorce from Dulcie, the woman he had impulsively married just over two years ago. And then separated from six weeks later. It had been a spectacular, uncharacteristically reckless act of self-harm. Fortunately, its brevity meant that no one in his family knew anything about it. Not even Carlo.

Far better if it stayed that way. He could get some anonymous lawyer to send her the paperwork, but wouldn't it be better, safer, more satisfying to do it in person?

And now that he thought about it, he couldn't quite understand why he hadn't sought legal closure before. There was no possibility of a reunion. Dulcie's rejection was so tangled up with his mother's savage words after Edo's death, he couldn't go there.

Couldn't prod that wound.

It would be far easier, far less painful to find a new wife, one who would do what Dulcie had so conspicuously failed to do.

CHAPTER ONE

BREATHING UNEVENLY, Dulcie Shaw slid through the door of the lecture theatre. The professor giving the lecture, Dr Claire Blake, was already speaking to the assembled students, and Dulcie sat down hurriedly on the last empty seat in the back row and opened her laptop.

She'd run all the way from the labs, and her heart was pounding so loudly she couldn't hear Dr Blake's voice but thankfully her notes would be available online.

Several rows closer to the stage, a young man with blond hair and a lazy gaze glanced over at her with a mixture of curiosity and disdain. He was an undergraduate. She recognised him from the labs. But it was unlikely he recognised her, she thought. Working as a lab technician was like having the power of invisibility.

She didn't dislike the undergraduates. Most, especially the girls, were polite in that awkward way of people recognising their privilege and wanting to apologise for it. Some simply ignored her. They were mostly male and, even without exchanging a word, she knew they had been raised in homes and schools where the women who cooked and cleaned and applied plasters to scuffed knees were not the kind of women who mattered enough to notice.

They were the kind of men who had a compartmentalised life. They were binary in their thought processes. For them, and, in consequence, for those who crossed their path, life was a flow chart of clear, simple choices.

Me or your mother.

Me or your brother.

Her shoulders stiffened. Because clear and simple didn't have to mean those choices were fair or right. Sometimes the act of choosing was wrong.

Of course, she was generalising. Not all men were like that. Maybe it was just her father and her husband. But it would be a long time before she tested that theory because, after what had happened with Ettore, she had sworn off dating.

Before him, she had always been careful to keep her relationships on a casual footing. She'd told the men she'd dated that she didn't like labels, but the truth was even letting someone hold her hand had felt as if she were putting it into a snare.

She'd got away with it because, thanks to her father's decision to send her to an expensive boarding school, she knew how to smile, to sparkle on command. She'd danced and giggled. And then she'd moved on.

Before things had got too deep or too complicated. Before they had got close enough to have power over her. She couldn't let that happen. Couldn't trust anyone to have that power. Power corrupted. It damaged lives. Wrecked relationships. Safer to stay single or travel light.

And then she'd met Ettore Marchesi. Thick dark hair, eyes the exact same colour as the bronze coins on display in the Fitzwilliam Museum up the road, and a sensual mouth that should have warned her to keep her distance.

'For those of you who are interested, I've added a link at the end of the lecture.' Dr Blake's voice snapped her attention back to the stage, and she stared fixedly at the screen.

Met.

The word popped into a bubble above her head as if she were a cartoon character.

It was such a small word to describe such a life-altering encounter. Meeting Ettore had been like atoms colliding to create an entirely new state of being. A state where hope and anticipation, and the excitement of sharing her life without borders and checkpoints, had felt normal. A state where she had been a different person. A Dulcie who had been confident in her choices.

And she had chosen him.

Chosen. Again, such an insipid word.

There had been no choice. Her need for him had been as inexorable and fierce and irresistible as a black hole.

Didn't stop it being a mistake.

She had trusted the wrong person. Again. Worse, she had trusted herself. And been burned. No skin graft had been required. There was no treatment other than the passing of time and, more critically, the avoidance of any further damage.

But that wasn't the only reason that stopped her from dating or even thinking about dating. Her eyes dropped to the third finger of her left hand. She didn't wear Ettore's ring any more. Not since he'd walked out of her flat and her life two years ago. But legally, they were still married.

Separated. Estranged. In limbo. But married.

And despite not having seen or heard from him since, frustratingly she still *felt* married.

It wasn't just the legality of it. Or the lack of definitive closure. She felt bound to him in other ways. Ways that she couldn't properly identify much less articulate to anyone. But then who would she articulate them to?

Since moving to Cambridge, she had colleagues rather than friends. Mainly because friends required a level of commitment that she simply couldn't give right now. Her limited free time was devoted to Oscar. Because her brother needed her. Because it was her fault that he was so fragile, so volatile. So damaged.

Her shoulders tensed as she remembered his outburst at the weekend.

'I knew you didn't want this. You've never wanted me in your life.'

He had been furious, shouting, smashing things and then tearful and scared, clinging to her, begging her not to leave, promising to change.

It was a cycle that had happened so many times already, often enough that she could sense it at a distance as an animal could sense a storm building unseen over a distant landscape. And it was her fault that Oscar was like this. She was the one who had left him with their alcoholic mother. She had abandoned him to an unstable, fractured childhood bouncing between children's homes and foster care. He was an addict because of what she'd done. And what she hadn't done.

She couldn't change the past. But she could atone. She could give Oscar the support and love he so badly needed. In the short term, that meant she needed to keep working, keep studying so she could finish her master's degree. Then she could get a better job that paid more money, and she would be able to get him some proper treatment.

That was her longer-term goal, although, truthfully, he needed treatment now. But supporting the two of them was already stretching her finances to near breaking point.

For the rest of the hour, she focused on Dr Blake, and fifty minutes later she was closing her laptop and following the other students down the stairs of the lecture theatre into the hallway. She wanted to ask the professor a question but there were so many students, and they all seemed to be dawdling like drivers on a motorway looking at a crash on the other side of the carriageway.

What were they looking at?

She stood on her toes, trying to see over their heads, mentally rolling her eyes as she saw that it was just some random man. He had his broad muscular back to her so she couldn't see his face, but he must be good-looking, she thought as a group of young women slowed to glance over their shoulders as they passed by, their eyes widening in appreciation.

Curiosity piqued her. She knew most of the staff at the college, and, even though he was standing with his back to her, there was something familiar about the shape of his head.

As if he could sense her gaze, the man rubbed the back of his neck, and she felt a flicker of recognition roll over her skin.

He must be a visiting lecturer. Probably he was waiting for Dr Blake, but as the professor got close enough to speak to him, she pulled out her phone and started talking.

'Hey, do you mind?'

Dulcie scowled up at a group of young men as they shoved in front of her, hemming her in with their rucksacks and shoulders, their extra height and width momentarily blocking the man from view.

And then suddenly they were stepping to the side of the corridor one after the other as if there was an obstacle in their path or some unseen hand was forcing them to move out of the way.

Five seconds later she saw what it was.

Or rather who it was.

The man was walking towards her, cutting through the mass of students, who turned towards him, their faces tilting up like flowers drawn to the sun. And at first, she was so distracted by their reaction that she didn't even look at him, and then, when she did, what she felt was not recognition but pure, unfiltered admiration.

Just as she had that first time when she saw him at Charles de Gaulle airport in Paris.

She could still remember it now. It was the end of a stressful and ultimately fruitless day. The storm that had been brewing over the city for days had escalated suddenly overnight, unleashing a ferocious deluge of rain before pounding the city with marble-sized hailstones. Travel around and out of the city had ground to a halt. Her flight, all flights, had been cancelled, and the concourse was crowded with refugees from the storm staring up at the blank departures board as if they could conjure up a plane by the power of thought alone.

Everyone looked tired and crumpled, including her, and she had been contemplating a coffee, but the queue was already curving across the concourse like the tail of a depressed cat.

And then, there he was, moving towards her with the muscular grace of a bigger cat, a puma or a jaguar.

Time had stopped. Or that was what it felt like. The edges of the vast room had blurred and everything inside that space was suddenly crisply outlined as if he were the eye of the storm.

And then, as now, every single person had turned to look at him.

Because he was beautiful. Tall, with dark, unkempt hair and a soft, shimmering bedroom gaze that was at odds with his calm, unswerving certainty.

A calm that was nothing like the volatile, emotional tinderbox of her childhood.

She was captivated. As powerless to resist as a moth to the phototactic pull of a flame. Which was why she was still standing there, frozen, mesmerised as he stopped in front of her, his dark coat flecked with glittering droplets of water, a cup of coffee in his outstretched hand.

She should have run a mile. An ultramarathon.

But instead, she had shared a taxi with him to a hotel in the South Pigalle. They had booked into separate rooms but by the following morning she had given him the ultimate power to hurt her. She had given him her heart.

And now, after years of silence and attrition, Ettore was back.

She breathed in sharply, and the jarring improbability of meeting him here, now, was as shocking as if he had upended a bucket of ice-cold water over her head.

She wasn't expecting this. Him. Ettore.

More disconcertingly she wasn't expecting to feel a sudden and disconcertingly fierce flicker of heat flare up inside her as if she were a match striking against powdered glass.

Which was why she was still forming sentences in her

head when he stopped in front of her, his striking light-coloured eyes resting on her face. Except that now there was a coolness there that jarred almost as much as the handmade leather shoes and the gold signet ring on his pinkie finger.

He had always dressed well. She had teased him about it when they were together. But back then they were equals. Now, she was working as a lab technician and a cleaner to pay her bills, and he had clearly moved up a level.

'Hello, Dulcie.'

She flinched inside. Hello, Dulcie? Seriously? Her heart jerked against her ribs as his words reverberated inside her head.

The last time he had spoken to her had been to ask her to choose between himself and her brother. Correction: he had made her choose. Even though she had begged him not to. But he had been insistent, a cold-eyed stranger.

So, she had chosen Oscar. How could she not?

Ettore hadn't tried to change her mind. He had simply turned and walked away. Because he could. Because he was looking for a reason to walk away. Because what they shared was not, as she'd thought, the real thing, but a mistake. He hadn't thought it worth his time to elaborate as to which of those explanations was correct. Hadn't thought Dulcie worthy of an explanation. He was too busy rewriting history, assigning the responsibility for their failed relationship to her.

And then he was gone. Because men like Ettore Marchesi and her father didn't own their failures. They lied and twisted the situation so that up was down. Black was white. Look at how her father had twisted the facts about her mum not wanting her. By the time she had learned the truth her mum was dead and Oscar was on a path to chaos and addiction.

'Her situation has changed,' he'd said. 'There's no place for you in her life any more.'

She had thought her mum had remarried. And her dad had never contradicted her. The truth was that her mum had been drying out in a clinic. But her father hadn't wanted to tell her that because then he would have had to tell her that Oscar was in care, and she would have wanted her brother to come and live with them instead.

Finding that out, she had felt like a bird hitting a window. She had been stunned, confused, scared.

Watching Ettore leave, she had felt like that same bird having its wings torn off. She had been stunned, wounded. Terrified of losing him for ever. But she hadn't gone after him. Then again, he hadn't returned. So, they were even, kind of.

No, they weren't, she thought savagely a moment later. They weren't even close.

Tilting up her chin, she met his gaze. 'What are you doing here?'

His light brown eyes glinted beneath the overhead lights but there was no softness there as he stared down at her.

'What, no "hi, there", no "how have you been?" or "it's good to see you"?' he said slowly. 'That's not much of a welcome.'

She glared at him. 'If you wanted a parade, you should have called me. Oh, but you haven't called, have you? Not once in two years. Not ever.'

'To be fair, you changed your number. And your name. Whose name is it, by the way?'

His expression didn't alter but there was a husky softness to his voice that made her shiver. He was annoyed, confused, angry even. And she could see why he would feel all and any of those emotions. When she and Ettore met, she was called Turner, but after he walked out on her she was done with taking the name of yet another man with a twisted world view of what love and loyalty should look like. She and Oscar had chosen the name Shaw together because she wanted there to be a connection that was theirs alone. To reassure him that she wasn't going anywhere.

Although she'd rather gouge out her own eyes than share those facts with Ettore.

'It's mine. Not that it's any of your business.'

'It is if you're committing bigamy.'

Her pulse thudded in her throat. She stared at him in disbelief.

Had he erased their disastrous marriage from his brain? Did he really think she could just pick out a new life with some other man and carry on living it concurrently with this one? 'You have to be joking. The last thing on my mind is another trip down the aisle, even with the added thrill of breaking the law at the same time. But given that you've managed to track me down, I'm guessing you already know I'm not committing bigamy. How did you find me, by the way?'

He shrugged, and it was annoying on so many levels that he was the only person who could lift his shoulders like that without looking like some sulky adolescent.

'Everyone can be found, Dulcie. It's not that hard.'

Could they? She felt a pang of guilt. After she'd found that correspondence between her father and the Children and Family Court Advisory and Support Service, and realised that Oscar had been in care, she had tried to find him. But for her, at least, it had been a frustrating and time-consuming process.

Hating him for instantly and unknowingly diminishing her, she scowled. 'You know what else isn't hard? Crawling back under whatever rock you've been living under.'

Ettore's eyes narrowed, and she felt the provocation of that remark ripple through him and beyond him into the sunlit street. But he didn't lose his temper. Instead, he stared at her assessingly, as if she were a painting he was thinking about buying.

'You have a choice.' His tone was pleasant but there was no mistaking the steel and warning in his voice. 'We can stand here trading childish insults or we can go somewhere more private and talk like adults.'

'If you came here to talk, you've wasted your time,' she said, breezily, her gaze fixed on the door to the street outside, and freedom from Ettore and his unexpected, unwelcome presence. 'There's nothing to talk about because, as far as I'm concerned, nothing has changed since we last met.' She sidestepped past him and pushed open the door, blinking into the sunlight.

In relation to their marriage, that was true. But some things had changed. She had bought a new house, a tiny two-up two-down that the estate agent had called a 'doer-upper'. So far, she had not done much to it other than paint the walls, but it had its own front door and a garden. On a less positive note, she had lost her job and become a nun, albeit unofficially.

'You're right. It hasn't.'

Ettore was walking beside her now, matching his stride to hers, and she wanted to scream but Oscar had already been given a warning for causing a disturbance. The last thing he needed was for his sister to end up at the police station too.

'Do you mind?' She spun round to face him and instantly regretted it because it hurt, it hurt in a visceral way to look at him.

'We're still husband and wife.'

The tight focus of his gaze made her feel suddenly breathless, and then poundingly furious with herself for being so susceptible to what she knew better than anyone was just words.

They were husband and wife. She knew that, obviously, and yet hearing him say it out loud in this narrow, high-walled street within earshot of several complete strangers made her feel suddenly light-headed.

Easing back into the shadows of the college wall, she pressed her hand casually against the cool stone to steady herself and then shrugged.

'We're separated. We've been separated for two years.'

'Which is why I want to talk to you about our marriage.'

For a moment she couldn't breathe.

So that was why he was here. He wanted a divorce. And why would he want a divorce? She could think of only one reason, and despite herself, despite how badly she wanted not to care, the knowledge that Ettore had found someone else, someone to take her place, made a lump of misery swell in her throat.

If only she had got her act together and ambushed him

on some Italian side street. Catching him off guard and making him feel small and stupid and superfluous. He had walked out of her life two years ago. So, why hadn't she done so?

Why hadn't she tracked him down and demanded a divorce?

Her throat tightened. It was a simple enough question, but the answer was a little more complicated.

At first, his leaving hadn't felt real. Shock had paralysed her. Then she'd waited, hoping, yearning for him to get in touch. Which of course he hadn't. Hope had faded, to be replaced by an anger and a despair that had scared her with their intensity and magnitude and so she had buried her feelings, buried the past. Which was easier than it sounded because nobody knew she was married, not even Oscar.

Now though, Ettore had turned up with a spade and started digging.

'If by talking about our marriage, you mean ending it, you could have just emailed. I would have got around to it myself sooner or later, but our marriage was over so quickly I forgot all about it.'

He didn't like that, she thought, watching his eyes narrow, but, hey, cry me a river and screw him.

'But that's the point. I don't want to forget about it.'

His eyes grazed her face, watching her reaction. She had loved that before. That he had been so focused on her, so attuned to the infinitesimal shifts in her body and mood. Now though, she hated it. Worse, she was confused. 'I don't understand—'

'I didn't come here to get a divorce, Dulcie. I came here to remind you that we are still married.'

The simplicity of that statement sent shivers down her spine. Now she was even more confused. She crossed her arms, to stop the feeling that she was unravelling in the street.

'Why would you come all this way to remind me of that?'

There was a pause, and she got the feeling that Ettore was processing a dozen answers to that question.

'Because,' he said, at last, 'I believe it would be in both our interests for us to stay married. Not like this. Not living in different countries. But under one roof. I want you to come back to Italy with me. To Puglia.'

CHAPTER TWO

DULCIE STARED AT Ettore in shaken silence, sharply aware of the cool paving stones beneath her feet and the breath bottling in her throat. She knew her face was showing her shock and confusion, and she felt horribly exposed.

Because it wasn't just shock and confusion she was feeling. A part of her, a tiny, shaming, ridiculous part, felt something like hope or relief that he wanted her still.

'Not for ever, you understand. Just for the immediate future.'

She blinked, flinched inside.

Stupid Dulcie. Of course, he hadn't meant for ever.

Her shame engulfed her and maybe she made some kind of sound because his eyes narrowed on her face, and she felt her cheeks start to burn. She was such an idiot. Of course, Ettore didn't want her. She had been a summer fling. Was meant to stay a summer fling. That was how it had been every other year before Ettore. Most years, by the time summer ended, there had been many such flings. None had overstepped the mark.

All had been easy to give up.

Except him. Ettore Marchesi, the man standing in front of her, telling her in a cool, matter-of-fact voice that he wanted to stay married for the 'immediate future' because apparently it was in both their best interests to do so.

A stiletto blade slid between her ribs, the pain so sharp that she almost lost her balance. Two years ago, she'd thought their lives would be entwined for ever. She was his, and he was hers. Unconditionally.

Until he'd forced her to choose between him and Oscar, the brother she had failed to choose all those years ago.

Actually, make that just failed.

Her heart felt as if it were being squeezed in a vice as she remembered a two-year-old Oscar, with his huge, worried blue eyes and his small, sticky hand reaching for hers, climbing into her bed to the distant but audible soundtrack of their parents screaming at each other downstairs.

The marriage had limped on for far too long. Secretly, a part of her had longed for it to end so that the shouting would stop. So that their house, her home, didn't feel as if it were sitting on top of a fault line.

When her mother had called her into the kitchen and told her that she and her father were splitting up, her first feeling had been relief.

And then her father had asked her to choose who she wanted to live with.

It was an impossible, inappropriate question for a child to answer and she had been tongue-tied with panic because, even as a seven-year-old, she'd known that if her father left without her, none of them would see him again. If she was being generous, she told herself that was why she'd chosen him.

But if she was being truthful, she had chosen her father because her mother was an alcoholic and she hadn't wanted to be responsible for her.

Pushing the thought away, she took an unsteady step backwards.

'And that's why you came to find me.' Her voice was starting to spiral and, over Ettore's shoulder, she could see people glancing over curiously. It reminded her of when her mother had been drunk and she'd fallen over in the supermarket and everyone had stood frozen, watching her flail about on the floor.

Dulcie's heart thudded jerkily inside her chest. She had that feeling of a wave building, rising behind her to block out the light. She'd had that feeling so many times in her life. Of things getting impossibly big and beyond her ability to manage.

But not today.

'Let me think.' She pressed her finger against her forehead. 'You know what? I don't need to think. Obviously, I'm not interested in playing some weird marital charade with you. I don't know why you would even ask that question.'

'Then let me tell you.' He spoke quietly but there was an authority to his voice.

'No.' At the margins of her vision, she saw a man turn to stare at her. But she didn't care. Nor did she want to hear Ettore's reasons. Didn't he understand how cruel it was to ask her to do that? 'Our marriage is over. I thought I'd made that clear the last time we met.'

She made as if to step past him, but he moved neatly to block her escape and she felt a sudden suffocating panic. Not because she thought he would hurt her. Ettore had been passionate in bed, and he was physically strong, but even when provoked by Oscar, he hadn't hurt her brother, just restrained him.

But he was too close. So close that she could see the faint trace of stubble on his strong jaw. So close that she could feel the sheer, unfiltered maleness of his lean, muscular body. Close enough that she could remember the way he would roll her over to straddle him, his hands moving with devastating precision over her skin until she was just a pulsating, helpless extension of his body.

She blanked her mind, irritated at her brain's disloyal and baffling ability to focus on the good when there was so much more of the bad.

'Obviously, I'm not expecting you to make up your mind now. I understand it's a big decision to take so I'm happy to give you twenty-four hours to think it over. I'm staying at the Conisbrough in London—'

'I don't care where you're staying. And I don't need twenty-four hours. You could give me twenty-four years, and my answer would be the same. Whatever it is you're selling, I'm not interested in buying it.' *Caveat emptor.* Buyer beware. She had bought into love with Ettore and been burned.

'I'm not selling you anything, Dulcie. I'm offering you the chance to get your life back on track. And not just your life. Oscar's too. I know he's struggling and that you're supporting him. But can you give him the help he needs? Because I can. I can make that a reality.'

'You leave my brother out of this.' She was instantly, fiercely protective, shaken too that he knew so much about their lives. Though still not afraid of him.

His face was hard then, the bones like granite beneath the skin. 'As I remember, it was you that put him front and centre and above all others.'

Not always, she hadn't, and she would regret that for the rest of her life.

'You don't know anything about my brother or me—'

'I know that he's still drinking. Still violent. That he lost you your job—'

'He's not violent!' Oscar got loud and incoherent when he was scared and he threw things and smashed them, but he had never hit anybody, never hurt her.

Not intentionally, and only that one time when he and Ettore first met.

Her pulse slowed as Ettore's words replayed inside her head and then she frowned. 'How do you know that? About my job?' Her eyes narrowed on his face. 'Have you been spying on me?'

His jaw tightened. It was something that she had never quite managed to understand, that way he had of suddenly putting distance between himself and other people. It was as if a barrier had risen up like that privacy screen in the limo her friend Dina had hired for her hen night. In the past, it had happened sometimes when they were out in a restaurant or in the street when someone got too messy or too loud.

But never with her. Never when they were alone.

It made her feel slightly sick, knowing that she was now someone he wanted to keep at arm's length.

'Not spying, no. I was trying to find you. So that we could have this conversation. You'd changed your number and your address, so I went to where you were working. Where you used to work, as it turned out.'

Staring down at Dulcie's taut face, Ettore managed to hold onto his temper. In part, that was only possible because he was still reeling from his abrupt, inexplicable volte-face.

He had come to Cambridge fully intending to tell Dulcie that he wanted a divorce. He had the paperwork in his pocket, more for effect than any legal requirement. But then he had seen her outside the lecture theatre, and everything he had planned to say had been overridden. In fact, he had gone a step further and, instead of demanding a divorce, he had suggested the opposite. And now he couldn't backtrack without looking either stupid or unhinged.

Which quite frankly felt like a fair assessment of his current behaviour. He couldn't recall when he'd ever acted so impulsively.

Not true, he thought, remembering his humbling scamper across Charles de Gaulle airport, a coffee cup in his outstretched hand.

Meeting Dulcie Turner in a rare moment of freedom had felt like serendipity and salvation all rolled into one. Marrying her two months later had been a spur-of-the-moment impulse, a random act of recklessness in a considered, constricted life.

With her sparkling smiles and her love of the natural world, Dulcie was the complete antithesis of the cool, metropolitan women he'd dated in the past. Women like him, who had a role to play. She tasted like freedom and possibility. She was sunshine and sherbet on his tongue.

The intensity of his attraction had overruled common sense and the whole unassailable inappropriateness of his response to her.

And now it had happened again. She had turned him into a creature of impulse.

He swore silently. How the hell was he going to explain this turn of events to his family? To Carlo?

But explaining away the unexplainable, the unreasonable, the irrational was his superpower.

'They had no right to tell you why I left.'

'People like to gossip,' he said obliquely. 'And no doubt your brother's antics helped break up an otherwise boring day.' No need to mention that people particularly liked to gossip when there was a financial incentive to do so.

He watched a flush of colour seep across her cheeks. She was angry and hurt, but what of it?

She had no idea what it had been like walking out of her flat into the darkness. He had found sleep impossible. Eating, a chore.

The accident had added despair and shame to his misery. He had missed her so badly and had stopped taking the pain medication because he had been paranoid that he might mention her name, call out for her.

And no amount of morphine could dull the pain of losing both Dulcie and Edo.

It had been the one time in his life that he'd been grateful for his family's telenovela tendencies. Grateful for anything that would distract him from that ache inside.

'They don't know the full story.' She glowered at him.

That old chestnut, he thought, and he felt a stab of frustration. How many times had his brother or his father or his cousins trotted out that line when the consequences of their antics had needed to be quietly and discreetly swept under a particularly large and forgiving carpet?

It might not be the full story but, in his experience, there was no smoke without fire.

Besides, he had met her brother. He was a definite firestarter, he thought, picturing Oscar's glazed eyes and curling lip when they had found him waiting on the doorstep of Dulcie's flat.

'Of course, I wouldn't have had to go to your workplace if you hadn't changed your name,' he said softly.

Her chin jerked up, blue eyes wide like a Siamese cat.

But why Shaw?

There was no obvious explanation. Nor was it of any concern to him. And yet it needled him. That she should prefer any name to his.

And solitude to his company, he thought a moment later as she darted sideways and, this time, she made it past him and he found himself in the incredible position of having to pursue her down the street, without actually looking as if he was pursuing her because the last thing he needed was to make a scene.

'You can't keep running away from this, Dulcie.' He was walking beside her just as he used to do whenever they went out together. Only then they used to hold hands and now her hands were curled into tight fists. 'More importantly, there's no point. I know where you live.'

'So, you're a stalker now. And you wonder why I don't want to accept your tempting offer of marriage?'

'I'm not offering to marry you. We're still married.'

'Barely,' she snapped. 'And not for much longer. The sooner we get divorced, the better.'

'There was nothing stopping you from filing for divorce when you ended our marriage.'

'I didn't end our marriage.' She stopped so abruptly and he was walking so fast that he was several feet ahead of her before he realised that she had stopped and he was forced to stride back to her. 'You did. You made me choose.'

Her blue eyes were narrowed now, reminding him even more of an angry feline.

'And you chose your brother.'

She squared up to him, her ponytail flicking provocatively from side to side in a way that made him want to reach out and grab it and wrap it around his hand and tether her to him, and he had a sudden, dangerous urge to step closer, and keep stepping closer.

'Because you made it a choice. And now you're trying to force me to make another choice.'

Now she was walking again, and he was having to lengthen his stride to catch up with her.

'I'm merely asking you to do something you did two years ago of your own volition. You are my wife.'

She stopped next to a bike, chained to some railings. 'I haven't been your wife since you walked out of my flat in London, two years ago, Ettore. And according to our vows, I never was. I mean, you didn't exactly follow through on for better or worse, did you? You met my brother, and you judged him, and you found him wanting. And you expected me to validate your judgement. And that was why our marriage ended.'

Not true, he thought furiously. But the past, their past, was history. The real-time equivalent of a closed book. What mattered was the present and the immediate future. And the narrative arc that required him to be married.

'Because you cared about your brother more than our marriage. And yet, when it comes to it, when you have an opportunity to make his life better, you won't take it. I can make his life better. Yours too.'

He watched as she crouched down to unlock the padlock. 'My life is fine. More importantly, it's here. What possible reason would I have to give it all up for you?'

It was tempting to point out that moments earlier she had refused to listen to his reason for doing so. Instead, he said, calmly, 'If you agree to my proposal, you'll need to give up your jobs so naturally I will recompense you. And I will be generous, enough for you to get Oscar real, professional help.'

Her chin snapped up. 'You're going to pay me? To be your wife.'

He could feel her shock, greater even than when he had suggested that they stay married. And he could feel her retreating inside herself, to that place that he had never managed to access. Because that was where Dulcie had failed their marriage vows.

She might have promised 'to have and to hold' but for him that had meant fully and completely accepting him, committing to him, recognising his needs and being present for him, and that had been true sexually, but emotionally she had always kept a part of herself out of reach.

Now though, it felt as though she had raised the drawbridge and closed the portcullis.

'That's very "generous" of you, Ettore. But as being your wife would mean having to spend time with you, I'd rather scrub toilets for the rest of my life. Don't come looking for me again. Now you know where I live, you can just send me the divorce papers. Ciao, Ettore.' She mounted the bike and before he could reply she was pedalling furiously away from him, her blonde ponytail streaming behind her as she bumped over the cobblestones and out of his life for the second time.

But this time, he was not letting her go.

* * *

Later, Dulcie would wonder how she had got home. She had no memory of stopping at any traffic lights or turning left or right. The last memory she had was of twisting the dials on her padlock with trembling fingers.

And Ettore's beautiful, so familiar face, not soft with love, but dark with frustration as she cycled away.

Unlocking her front door, she bumped her bike's wheel over the threshold and into the hallway. Her heart was racing, not from the speed at which she had pedalled. It was the shock of seeing Ettore again. And of his offer—suggestion, proposal? Whatever it was—to stay as his wife. For money.

Her head swam and she leaned back against the wall, breathing in the cool, still air of the tiny house she had bought eighteen months ago. She and Oscar had repainted it with various calming shades of green and pulled up the horrific carpets. Now there were varnished floorboards and rugs, and a sofa dotted with cushions.

She had wanted it to be a home for Oscar. But the truth was, she had no idea how to make a home.

When she was a child, her family's house was large and full of material possessions, but it also quivered with a claustrophobic tension, a kind of permanent sense of impending doom. After her parents' divorce, she lived in a bigger house filled with even more material possessions. But her father was critical and controlling. He paid for everything, but he wanted results, and he didn't tolerate flaws or weaknesses or defiance.

As she remembered their last conversation, her breathing stumbled.

Her father was no role model, any more than her mother had been.

But maybe she was doing something right because Oscar had been doing so much better lately. He was doing exercise and even volunteering for two hours every day. A sense of purpose was part of the programme that she and Oscar had agreed with his counsellor. That and a curfew. Which he hadn't missed for over two months now.

She was so proud of him. Of both of them. They were a family with their own unique name. They didn't need anyone else. Although it was an undeniable bonus that Oscar liked their neighbours, Chris and Kelly.

She needed to focus on that, on Oscar, and forget Ettore's ridiculous, incomprehensible proposal.

Ridiculous because they had managed only six weeks of married life the last time, and incomprehensible because she hadn't given him a chance to explain his reasons for wanting to stay married.

Because he had offered her money.

'If you agree to my proposal, you'll need to give up your jobs so naturally I will recompense you.' With an effort, she blanked out the memory of Ettore's voice.

Focus, she told herself firmly.

Oscar would be leaving work any time now and regular meals were another part of his recovery.

Twenty minutes later, Dulcie was cooking in the kitchen when she heard the soft thump of the front door closing. Glancing at the clock on the oven, she smiled. Oscar was early.

'I'm in the kitchen,' she called out. 'We're having your favourite. I even added cream to the mashed potatoes.'

'That's great.'

Her scalp froze and the contents of her stomach solidified into a hard, unyielding lump. She turned slowly away from the saucepan on the hob. But she didn't need to. She recognised that note. Over the last three years, she had grown attuned to every tiny shift in her brother's speech and behaviour patterns.

Someone else might not even have noticed the slight slur that he was trying to conceal in his voice. But she could hear it, and she knew what it meant.

Carefully, she put the masher in her hand down on the counter. 'What did you take?'

He blinked, doing confusion, but his pupils were like pinpricks, the blue of the irises huge and glassy. 'I don't—'

'Yes, you do, Oscar. We've been here before, remember?' How could either of them forget? The first few times it had happened she had comforted herself by thinking, It's only the second time. Or the fifth or tenth. Then she'd stopped counting.

'Because you can't forget. Because you think I'm a failure.' He was all fast breath and twitching limbs now; a puppet being pulled in multiple directions by the cocktail of drinks and drugs he'd taken. 'You think I'm like Mum. That's why you left me—'

And so it went on, following a predictable and exhausting pattern.

The first stage was denial, quickly followed by a savage and disbelieving anger at her lack of faith and her utterly predictable but unjustified refusal to believe in him, which segued into a tearful critique of her character. En route, all the cutlery and plates she'd laid out for dinner were swept violently onto the floor and he threw the vintage cine camera she'd given him for his birthday across the room.

As the sausages started to burn, the smoke alarms broke into an insistent, ear-splitting screech and Oscar covered his ears and crouched on the ground, crying incoherently.

Five hours later, she had thrown away the charred sausages and congealed mashed potato and swept up the broken glass and plastic and china. Oscar was curled up foetus-style on the sofa, his fist pressed against his mouth, moaning occasionally as his breath deepened into sleep.

Dulcie watched him from the armchair, clutching a cushion. She hadn't gone to bed. There was no point because she knew she wouldn't and shouldn't sleep deeply. Instead, she ate some crackers and drank a glass of water. She was exhausted but also on high alert. With an effort of willpower, she forced herself to count the plus points.

He had come home to her.

He hadn't stormed off.

And he didn't need to go to A & E.

As plus points went, it was a pretty sad list, she thought, trying to swallow past the lump in her throat. She felt old, like really old. Her body ached with sadness and shame.

It wasn't enough. She wasn't enough to save him.

Three years ago, when she had found him in a seedy flat near Brixton prison, she had hoped that she would be. That she might be able to transfer all the benefits that she'd been gifted by the life she had chosen at the age of seven. The life she had denied her brother.

But Oscar's problems were so deep rooted. He'd had

two decades of chaos and poverty and neglect. And a decade of addiction.

'I know he's struggling and that you're supporting him. But can you give him the help he needs? Because I can.'

Ettore's words were so loud inside her head that she almost jumped out of her skin, and she had to hug the cushion tightly to steady herself.

The trouble was, much as she wanted to deny it, Ettore was right. Even with her support, Oscar's grip on reality was loose-fingered at the best of times. What he needed was long-term, residential rehabilitation. But that was big money. More money than she earned.

Only what would happen if she did nothing? If she just kept trying to stitch therapy and rehab together into a haphazard quilt as she'd been doing for months now? Years, she corrected herself.

What if he got worse? What if he did what their mother did?

She had waited long enough. She wasn't going to lose Oscar because of her pride. He needed proper care, and she would do anything to make sure he got it.

Even if it meant living under the same roof as her estranged husband.

CHAPTER THREE

STARING UP AT the Conisbrough Hotel in Belgravia, Dulcie felt her heart relocate to her throat.

It was just over nineteen hours since Ettore had made his proposal.

Or issued his ultimatum, depending on how you looked at it. Aside from when they were both asleep, most of those intervening hours had been spent trying to convince Oscar that she wasn't leaving him and that he hadn't wrecked everything and that she would be coming back.

And she understood why he needed that certainty. Knew that the root cause of his anxiety and insecurity was her fault. Which was why she had spent a long time reassuring him, giving him the certainty he needed. Now though, as she walked across the polished black and white marble floor, she wished she had someone who could make her feel certain that she was doing the right thing.

For Oscar.

For herself.

It didn't help that there were so many parallels to the last time she had stepped out of her day-to-day life. And then, as now, she was travelling to meet Ettore.

The difference was that two years ago she hadn't known she would be meeting him.

The memory of that first time she saw him snapped into focus. As a scientist, she had always thought that being swept off your feet was hyperbole. But that was before the dark-haired man with the eyes of a lion had cut a swathe through the crowds milling beneath the departure board.

She had wanted to laugh.

Later, after he'd walked out of her flat without a backward glance, she'd wanted to cry. But she hadn't gone after him.

Her legs had overruled her heart, refusing to let her make the same mistake as she had at aged seven. It didn't matter that watching him leave felt like open heart surgery without an anaesthetic. Choosing to put your life in the hands of someone who demanded you sacrifice some part of yourself to earn their love was a slower, equally painful death of sorts.

And yet, here she was in London, to take up his offer and go to Puglia with him as his wife.

The idea made her feel like a biplane in a tailspin. Everything was moving so fast. Too fast for her to keep her thoughts from blurring. But one thing stayed still and clear-edged. Oscar needed help. Professional help. And all she needed to do to make that happen was something she had already done, willingly, eagerly—

So eagerly that the memory of it felt almost alien. As if it had happened to someone else. Or as if she'd been someone else entirely. Someone she neither recognised nor understood. As much of a stranger as those two random people they had tugged into the Marylebone register office to witness their wedding.

It had been the simplest of ceremonies. The perfect

postscript to a fairy-tale romance. And her love for Ettore had been utterly unprecedented in its purity. Before, with her family, her love for her parents had been coloured by fear and anxiety. With Oscar, it was threaded through with guilt.

But this was her chance to atone properly. Maybe guilt was not enough of an offering to the gods. Maybe she had to suffer too.

Smiling at the doorman, she stepped in the foyer and pulled out her mobile phone. On the train, during one of the frequent occasions when she'd lost her nerve, she had dithered about simply calling the hotel and asking to speak to Ettore. She had even got her phone out and found the number. But if she was agreeing to stay as his wife, she was going to have to face him sooner or later. And this way she would catch him off guard.

Payback for how he'd ambushed her in the street.

Now, she pulled up the hotel's website. She had seen someone do this in a film once and it had all looked very easy but she felt all fingers and thumbs.

Holding her breath, she pressed the phone icon. There was a ringtone and then a male voice answered. 'Conisbrough Hotel, good morning, how may I help you?'

'Hi there.' She cleared her throat. 'Could you put me through to one of your guests? It's Mr Marchesi.'

'Of course. Just putting you through.'

Without waiting to hear the phone connect, she slipped it into her pocket, breathing out unsteadily. Now for the hard part.

She walked purposefully over to the reception desk, smiling as the young blonde receptionist looked up from her screen.

'Good morning, how may I help you?'

'Good morning. Mr Marchesi is expecting me. Could you put a call through to his room and tell him I'm here?'

'Of course.' The receptionist smiled and tapped her headset.

There was a bowl of roses on the countertop and, holding her breath, Dulcie leaned forward casually as if to inhale their scent. As she did so, her eyes darted to the screen on the desk. She had seen someone enact this whole scene in a film once. This was where the room number magically appeared on the screen, but she had no idea if it would work—

She blinked. It had.

Not a number, a name. The Royal Suite.

It had worked.

A rush of adrenaline burned through her like a tequila slammer so that it took her a moment to realise the receptionist was speaking to her.

'I'm sorry, the line was engaged.' The receptionist smiled apologetically.

'That's fine.' She rolled her eyes, doing blonde. 'I just realised, I have his mobile number, so I'll call him on that. But thank you.'

She melted backwards into a group of guests who had fortuitously appeared and then turned and walked over to the lifts as casually as she could manage. Her heartbeat sounded like horses' hooves thundering against her ribs. And as the lift doors closed behind her, she slumped back against the wall, relief momentarily swamping her panic.

Dulcie hadn't called.

Ettore flicked his cuff back to check his watch, again, and then stopped himself.

He didn't need to look at the time to know that it was running out.

Should he have followed her? Probably. Would it have changed anything? Almost certainly not. He had offered the biggest, juiciest bait—the chance to give Oscar real, long-term care. But Dulcie hadn't bitten.

On the contrary, instead of snatching his offer from his hand, she had fled from him. As for staying married, it appeared he had crystallised her determination to seek a divorce.

Good job, Ettore, he thought, dropping down into the leather armchair that offered unparalleled views of the Houses of Parliament and the London Eye. For a moment, he stared at the huge wheel. At this distance it was hard to believe it was moving. Almost as hard as it was to believe that it was two years since he had last seen it.

It had been a conscious choice to avoid visiting London. The idea of being in the same city as Dulcie and not being with her would have rubbed salt in an imperfectly healed wound.

But somehow, he doubted it would hurt more than seeing her in Cambridge had.

His shoulders stiffened as he pictured her hair streaming behind her like the tail of a kite as she cycled away from him. As for that 'Ciao' she had tossed in his face as you might toss a crust of bread to a pigeon. It was the first word he had spoken to her, and she had been amused by the fact that it could mean both hello and goodbye. Her use of it yesterday was deliberate, he was sure. Pointed even.

There was a knock at the door. In the next-door suite,

he heard his bodyguards get to their feet. But it was probably just housekeeping, and frankly he needed a distraction.

'It's fine,' he called out. 'I'll get it.'

He strode across the room and yanked open the door.

His jaw felt slack, and he knew that he must look surprised, but it wasn't just surprise he was feeling. Seeing Dulcie outside his room was giving him flashbacks to a different room in a different hotel in a different city when Dulcie had knocked on his door at three in the morning. Opening it, he had stared down at her face, his chest churning with hope and longing and then she had leaned in and kissed him and he had fallen into a parallel world. A world where for the first, the only time in his life he had been able to relax, to be who he wanted, to do what he wanted without needing to consider anyone but himself.

Was she remembering it too? Was she seeing the two of them in that half-empty hotel? Orphans of the storm. Strangers in the night.

Except they hadn't been strangers when morning came. Or that was what it had felt like. But then three months later it had turned out that he hadn't known her at all.

'Do you want to do this here?'

Perhaps Dulcie was remembering that night. There was a rough catch to her voice, and he was so distracted by it that his brain kept replaying her question like a needle hitting a scratch on a record. Do this? Do what?

'Or shall I come in?' Her second question, accompanied by a tilt of her head towards his suite, brought him back to his senses and, nodding, he took a step backwards.

'I think that would be best.'

As she stepped past him, he waited a few seconds to get his breathing back under control and then he followed her, closing the door softly and pulling out his phone to text his bodyguards that he didn't want to be disturbed.

'This is nice.'

Dulcie was walking slowly around the suite, her fingers grazing the smooth leather upholstery. She was dressed casually in jeans and a T-shirt, and her hair was tied back in a kind of half-up half-down arrangement that all women seemed to be able to do in their sleep. But there was a tension to her straight back, and he wondered if she was already regretting her decision to find him.

'Your family's business must be doing well.'

His shoulders stiffened, her words jarring. He was not a practised liar, but he was sometimes a pragmatic one.

Two years ago, he hadn't told Dulcie that he was the son of a duke or that his family owned a castle. And not only because, unlike the rest of his family, he rarely used his title. He'd learned that people changed when they found out those facts.

But his reasons for not telling her were more complicated than that. Shortly before they'd met and after years of simply playing at being the heir, Edo had decided he wanted to step up for real. In consequence and for the first time in what felt like for ever, Ettore had slipped the leash and his security detail and escaped to Paris.

His plan had been to be himself. To find out what that meant.

Instead, he'd found Dulcie.

And it had felt like fate. His mind had been made up. Marrying her was the impetus he'd needed to walk away from a life in a gilded cage that felt narrow and not his own. All they'd needed was each other. Only then Oscar had appeared, and his new wife's focus had switched to her brother, and he had panicked, and in his panic he had pushed her to choose between them.

She had chosen Oscar and ended their marriage.

And it had been as if some great foundation stone had been smashed. Two months later Edo and his mother had been in the family mausoleum, and it was his sister, Fia, who had left the castle. He had been left to pick up the pieces. He was still picking them up now.

But there was no need to share any of that with Dulcie. Some of it was beyond her pay grade and the rest she would find out after she had signed the relevant paperwork.

'It was a good year.'

He moved in the opposite direction to her, still keeping her at the edge of his vision, not crowding her as he had in Cambridge, giving her space. A planet orbiting a sun.

Years of managing his family had taught him better than any business qualification how to negotiate his preferred outcome but seeing Dulcie in Cambridge had made him forget everything he knew. All he had been able to think about was that she was there and that she was no longer his, and he had felt so angry and thwarted, and she had felt his anger and fled.

So now he waited. Made himself wait for her to bat the ball back over the net.

'So why do you need a wife?' She stopped abruptly, her eyes locking onto his, the blue of the irises bright and clean-edged like the feathers on a jay's wing. 'That is why you want to stay married to me, isn't it? And it must be something important to drag you all the way to England to come and find me. I mean, you've managed to avoid doing that for two years.'

She was smart. Smarter than many people probably gave her credit for, and by people he meant mostly men. Most likely they clocked the hair and the mouth and the curves.

He had, he thought, remembering the moment when she had stumbled into the airport with her suitcase wearing a pale blue cardigan and heeled sandals that had probably looked perfect for a late spring break in Paris but had been woefully inadequate for the unseasonal storm whipping its way through the city.

A storm had whipped its way through his body at the sight of the sodden fabric clinging to her skin. With her hair falling in wet strands over her shoulders and her unsteady gait, she had looked like a mermaid who had swapped her tail for legs.

And she had been holding a cuddly toy and all he'd been able to think was that he was too late. She'd had a baby. Had a partner.

She'd glanced up at the departure board, frowning, and he'd seen her shoulders rise and rise. And then she'd turned and scanned the concourse, her blue eyes narrowing on a distant coffee concession, then back to a passing air steward. Even at that distance he'd known her eyes would be the drowning blue of the ocean. He'd been on his feet and on his way towards her before he'd remembered he didn't know her.

Marrying her hadn't changed that fact.

It was only then that he realised that Dulcie was staring at him assessingly, and that he had no idea how much time had passed since she'd asked her question.

'My father is ill. He's an old man and his heart is failing. I can't change that. And he's had a good life.' A tumultuous life might be a better description. 'I think he would say that he has done everything he set out to do.'

'But he wants to see you married.'

Smart, he thought again.

He nodded.

It was easier to confirm a lie than to be the one to tell it in the first instance. But if he told her that he needed a wife to satisfy some ancient, irrational clause about inheritance it would simply throw up questions with answers that would lead onto more questions.

There was a sudden stiffness to her face.

'Then you're doing this for your father?' There was a bitterness to her voice, and he knew that she must be thinking about the choice he had thrust upon her two years ago.

But this wasn't just about his family. Letting the castle and the estate pass to his uncle or his cousins would be like setting fire to six hundred years of history. Not to mention the people who worked for him and relied on the estate for their income and, in some cases, their homes.

He had sympathy for Oscar, but Dulcie had instantly prioritised her brother over him, which hurt. It sounded petty, and it was, shamingly and uncharacteristically so. Because he was not a petty man. He had learned to live with his parents' favouritism for his siblings because you didn't choose your family. But what man could stand to be sidelined in his marriage?

'You think I'm a hypocrite.'

She didn't bother to disagree, just stared at him in silence. Then, after a long pause, she said slowly, 'I'm sorry. About your father.' She hesitated. 'Does he know about us? Was that why you came to find me? Was it his idea?'

Ettore felt his chest tighten. 'No.' He shook his head. 'He doesn't know.'

And really, what was there to know? He and Dulcie were married for five weeks and six days. And how was he to tell it? He didn't have the vocabulary to describe a marriage that had imploded without warning. Nor an inclination to share the truth. That his wife had chosen her family over him.

'It seemed a little indulgent.'

She blinked. 'Indulgent?'

'It would have stirred up a lot of questions and emotions for no reason. The marriage was over.' In truth, it had barely begun. 'Are you saying you told your family?' he said after a moment, his throat constricting.

Because she hadn't told Oscar. And she could have. They were still together then, still planning for a future.

Or perhaps she wasn't.

He could still remember the moment when he realised that she hadn't and didn't want to tell her brother that she was married.

'It's not the right time.' That was what she'd said after having introduced him to Oscar as her boyfriend, but if not then, when? It had been impossible to ignore, like a stone in a shoe. It was true that he hadn't told his family at that point but, clearly, he would have done so.

Dulcie's hesitation had made him question himself. He'd had to know for sure what he meant to her.

And she'd told him.

Now her gaze stayed steady, but her voice was scratchy when she answered. 'Like you said, there was no point. It was easier just to forget it ever happened.'

It: their marriage, and, by association, him.

'Until now,' she added, and their eyes locked.

'Until now,' he agreed.

'So how do you see this working?'

Good question, he thought. How did he see it working? But the answer was not something he had given much thought to until he'd opened his mouth yesterday and said something completely different from what he'd been planning to say.

'I suppose we would act as man and wife,' he said finally, a pulse beating in his hand as if his heart had momentarily relocated from his chest.

Man and wife. The words made him think of damp skin and soft lighting and a tangle of bedsheets and, gazing down at Dulcie, he saw that her pulse was beating in time with his and a flush of colour was contouring her cheekbones.

'In public,' he clarified, although there must be something wrong with him because it was hard not to stall his reply so he could watch a flush of pink seep down over the smooth pale underside of her jaw.

'In private, we would simply be ourselves.'

He had no idea what that meant but she let it pass.

'And the money?'

Given that it was his idea to pay her, her question stung more than it should, and he suddenly wished that he had never mentioned money.

He held her gaze. 'Do you have a figure in mind?'

'I thought you would. You're the one putting a price on our marriage.' She stared straight back into his eyes. 'Like you said, I'm going to have to give up my jobs and pay my rent. And I looked into the kind of clinics that do residential rehab, and the Dymphna Clinic looks like the best fit for Oscar. It's more expensive but I want the best for him.' Her eyes found his, blue, unblinking, challenging him to refuse. 'I'll let you do the maths.'

And perhaps there was something wrong with him because he would have paid ten times what it would cost him to get her to smile at him then.

'I can do that.'

'And just so we're clear, it's going to be a loan, not a gift. I'll set up a standing order to your account.' She stared at him steadily. 'It might take some time, but I'll pay back every penny.'

That stung too, more so than if she had accepted his money unquestioningly. Which made no sense whatsoever.

Clearly he was still processing her sudden change of heart. 'Anything else?'

She bit her lip. 'Then there's the marriage licence. How are we going to explain that we got married two years ago?'

'It's probably best if we stick as close to the truth as possible. Let's say that we argued and you stormed off—'

'I didn't storm off.' She frowned. 'We were in *my* flat—'

'Fine, then I will storm off in our "pretend" past.'

She lifted up her chin. 'Good. Because storming off suits you better. In our "pretend" past.' There was a rasp to her voice now. 'And then you realised you made a big mistake and came looking for me.'

Now it was his turn to shake his head. 'We bumped into one another by chance, and it all started up again.'

What exactly did he mean by 'it'? But he didn't need to ask the question.

He could feel 'it' skating over his skin and in the low thud of hunger in his stomach. And he was certain, without having any kind of proof, that Dulcie was feeling it too.

It had always been that way, their bodies communicating without language. But this wasn't their story, it was make-believe. And yet it felt real, and that faint tremor beneath her skin and the flush across her cheeks looked real too.

Because he knew her desire as well as he knew his own.

For a moment, they stared at one another, his pulse reverberating inside him so loudly he was surprised she couldn't hear it.

'And you think that's believable?'

There were pink smudges on her cheeks shaped like thumbprints, just as if he had touched her there, and for a few half-seconds they stared at each other in the shifting silence shimmering around their too tense bodies. And then he stepped closer, close enough that he could feel her warm breath and watch her eyes cling to him as he moved.

'It's not a question of whether I believe it. It either is or it isn't.'

'And is it?'

'Let's see, shall we?' he said, and he brought his mouth down on hers and he felt her body stiffen, her hands press against his chest except she wasn't pushing, she was pulling him closer. He felt his body harden and he parted her lips, deepening the kiss, his hand flattening against her spine, and he was on the verge of tilting her head back and moving to kiss her throat when he heard the sound of his bodyguards' voices in the adjoining room.

It was enough to shatter the spell he was under. Loosening his grip, he broke the kiss and Dulcie edged away from him, her blue eyes wide and shocked.

'I think we can pull it off, don't you?'

Without waiting for her response, he turned and walked over to a marble-topped console table and picked up an envelope. 'I have a contract for you to sign. Once it's signed, I'll transfer the money to your account. And you'll need a ring,' he added after a moment.

Her pulse nudged the skin at the base of her throat. 'I still have the one you gave me.'

She had?

The air seemed to thicken around him, and he wanted to ask her why. But he still had his ring too and cross-examining Dulcie might legitimately require him to explain his motives for hanging onto it. Better simply to move on.

'And I have the one you gave me.'

There was a beat of silence and then she said in that light, clear voice that he found so fascinating, 'So what happens now?' She had recovered her composure, but he could still see the faint flush of colour along her collarbone.

He took his time, wanting to enjoy the storm still swirling in her eyes. 'We restart our married life together,' he said softly.

And this time it would be on his terms.

CHAPTER FOUR

DULCIE FELT HER phone vibrate as she was standing in the queue of people for passport control at Brindisi airport.

Oscar.

Her muscles clenched around the knot in her stomach. But as she stared down at the screen, she saw that it was just her phone updating, and she felt the same churning mix of relief and guilt as she had back in England when she watched Oscar walk off with Elaine O'Neill, the director of the Dymphna Clinic.

He had turned and waved to her and smiled encouragingly. And she knew that it was where he needed to be. But she'd still had to curl her toes into her shoes to stop herself from running after him, and she had driven away with tears blurring her eyes.

After that, she'd spent what felt like the remainder of the day staring into her wardrobe and hating all the contents. She was going to Italy, so it would be warm. But what exactly did you pack for a fake second-chance romance?

If this reunion were real, she would probably be packing barely there lingerie, but it wasn't. As for outerwear, the last time she and Ettore had been together she had still been a student.

Back then, her clothes were jeans and tees and hoodies and the occasional sexy dress. She had smartened it up for work but then she'd lost her real job, and now she was back to being a part-time student with two jobs. But nobody cared what she wore under her lab coat. And the cleaning company provided a uniform.

But she could hardly wear either of those to meet Ettore's family and so she'd ended up rushing to the shops and panic-buying some summery dresses and shorts and the sandals that were currently rubbing her feet to ribbons.

'It's your turn.'

She looked up from her phone, frowning.

'Sorry,' she muttered to the woman standing behind her, and then she stepped up to the glass-fronted booth and held out her passport to the uniformed border control officer.

The woman glanced at her photo and then her face, her own face inscrutable. 'What is your purpose in visiting Italy?'

Her purpose?

Dulcie cleared her throat. 'Well, up until a week ago my husband and I were estranged. But his father is old, and his health is failing, and my husband wants to make him happy, so he came to find me, and he's going to pay for my brother to go into rehab and in exchange I'm going to pretend that we've got back together.'

The woman didn't so much as blink.

Unsurprisingly, given that Dulcie had only spoken those words inside her head.

Out loud, she said, 'I'm meeting my husband's family for the first time. They live in Puglia.'

The woman still didn't blink but her expression thawed a fraction. 'Have a pleasant trip.'

That seemed unlikely, Dulcie thought, her fingers tightening around the handle of her suitcase as she trundled towards the arrivals area. It would be a miracle if she and Ettore managed to pull off this charade. Two years ago, it would have been a breeze. But then two years ago it was real.

For her, anyway.

A pulse of panic skimmed across her skin as she glanced at the crowd of people hovering around the arrivals gate. Most were eagerly scanning the passengers and there was a sprinkling of men holding up white boards but none with her name.

Ettore had texted to say he would meet her at the airport, so where was he?

He had left London before her so that he could tell his father the 'happy news' in person. Which made a sort of sense. Edoardo Marchesi might desperately want to see his son married, but if Ettore turned up with a wife out of the blue obviously it would be something of a shock. And it seemed likely that Ettore would want to avoid playing marital charades on a plane for three hours. And for once, she completely understood his point of view.

She heard a noise somewhere between a sob and a gasp and she turned as a woman sidestepped past her to embrace an identical woman. Both were crying. Moments later a young, dark-haired man was spinning his girlfriend off her feet as their mouths fitted together hungrily.

Dulcie kept walking.

She could remember that hunger, those unanchored days when just seeing Ettore would make her senses grow muddied. It was like running a permanent fever. She felt shivery and urgent and there was that burning thing in her chest that she couldn't allow herself to name at first because she was too scared to do so. Love was a choice. A dangerous choice but then all choices were inherently dangerous in her experience.

Except with Ettore, there was no choice.

She'd been attracted to men in the past. Not many, not enough perhaps to generalise. But maybe it was enough because, with all of them, it had felt as if she was making a conscious decision. That what she'd felt was generic. A basic sexual need, a woman responding to a man. They hadn't been unique. And there had been no feeling of breathlessness, of losing control of herself. Always there had been that voice warning her, cautioning her to stay remote.

With Ettore, it had been like a rogue wave rising up and sweeping her out to sea. It had been fast and unstoppable, and it should have been frightening. She should have been scared. But she'd felt no fear and instead of fighting to get back to shore, she'd let herself be pulled under.

Like in his hotel room in London.

Her face felt scalded. No, that wasn't the same, was it? Lips tingling, she replayed the moment when Ettore had kissed her gently at first, then more deeply, drawing her against his body.

And she had kissed him back, her hands winding around his neck, slipping effortlessly, eagerly back into the taste and the heat of him.

It had obviously been just a performance. A rehearsal, almost. They had been alone. There had been nobody there to convince, and yet—

'Signora Shaw?'

'Yes.' She blinked, her feet stuttering to a sudden stop as a thickset man in a dark suit stepped forward. He wasn't holding a board, but he smiled stiffly and made a small bow, which seemed a little formal, but then, like most Europeans, Italians had specific language for informal and formal ways of greetings. Maybe the formal kind came with a bow.

'*Buongiorno.* Welcome to Apulia. My name is Carmine. There is a car waiting for you. May I take your bag?'

'Oh, yes. Thank you.'

Was Ettore not meeting her? Had he sent a car instead? She felt a flash of annoyance, and then a disappointment that confused and annoyed her even more.

'If you would like to come this way.'

She followed Carmine, not, as she expected, towards the front of the terminal building, but to a discreet door at the far edge of the concourse. He flashed some kind of security clearance to a bored-looking man in a uniform and now they were in another building. It was cool and quiet like the foyer of an upmarket hotel. It reminded her of the entrance to the Conisbrough, and she felt her feet falter and then she was blinking into the bright Italian sunshine—

And that was when she saw him.

He was leaning against a dark blue car. It was almost the same colour as her own car back in Cambridge. But this was a very different vehicle. It was muscular yet elegant with a strong, distinctive silhouette and a powerful stance that exuded a kind of understated strength and refined athleticism.

A bit like its owner.

Ettore shifted position, his head tilting back to acknowledge her, his gaze hidden beneath his sunglasses, but she felt his focus as she walked slowly towards him, trying to channel a convincing facsimile of wife-reuniting-with-her-husband energy. Except that, to her overstressed brain, it felt more like a scene from a film where someone was being released from prison.

So why did it feel as if she were walking towards her jailer?

At that moment he pushed away from the car and her whole body stiffened with awareness as he took off his sunglasses. As she met his speculative gaze, she saw herself through his eyes. Blonde hair swept in a loose bun. No make-up. A simple summer dress that she'd thought would be cool in the Italian heat but now looked hopelessly crumpled.

'I missed you, *cara*.'

She lifted her head and looked into his eyes and for a few half-seconds she forgot that they were only pretending. For a few half-seconds she believed him. And then she saw the coolness in his gaze, and she hated herself for being so stupid. Hated him for turning her back, even momentarily, into the woman she'd been two years ago.

Ettore reached out and took her hand and his touch snapped against her skin like an elastic band, and it took every ounce of willpower she had not to jerk it away as he pulled her closer.

'Thank you, Carmine. I've got it from here.'

She heard the boot of the car click shut and then, behind her, she felt Carmine melt away. And they were alone in the bright, cheerful Italian sunshine that seemed glaringly at odds with the disquiet in her stomach.

He released her hand, and she stepped backwards quickly, her fingers curling into a fist, trying to quell the tingling sensation in her fingers.

'Did you have a good flight?'

She nodded. Ettore had stumped up for business class, so it had been very civilised. More civilised than that kiss they'd shared back in London. The thought popped into her head uninvited and to distract herself she said, 'When you weren't at the gate, I thought maybe you'd changed your mind about meeting me.'

His gaze rested on her face, light yet intent. 'On the contrary, the drive will give us time to get our stories straight and get reacquainted.'

Reacquainted.

There were so many possible interpretations of that word that she couldn't fix on one. But they were all equally daunting. Hadn't they done that back in England via email?

A knot was tightening around her sternum like a rope around a cleat and she felt a sudden urge to tap on one of the tinted windows of the two black SUVs that were parked on the other side of the car park and ask them how much they would charge to take her to Fiana.

Or, better still, tell Ettore that she'd changed her mind. But the paperwork was signed. Oscar was at the Dymphna. She was just going to have to find a way to make this work.

She glanced at his car. 'Shall we get going, then?' Any fears she'd had about having to make polite conversation or, worse, rake over the past again were swiftly forgotten.

Firstly, it took all of Ettore's focus to edge the dark blue car through the mid-morning crush of mopeds and cars and buses and when he pulled off the motorway and the roads got narrower and the buildings further apart, she forgot about speaking. She was too busy staring at the Italian countryside.

She had been to Rome on a school trip and skiing in the Alps with her father, but this was a different Italy.

It was breathtakingly lovely. Low, undulating hills in every shade of green, patched with olive groves and vineyards and dotted with tiled-rooved houses. And above it all, a sky as flawlessly blue as a sapphire. After the narrow, stone-walled streets of Cambridge, it all felt so open and light.

'We're taking the scenic route. I hope you don't mind.'

Ettore's voice yanked her out of her trance, and she turned towards him, her ribs tightening infinitesimally as his gaze shifted from the road to her face. 'It's a slightly longer journey but we're in no rush and it will give you a chance to see the country.'

His country. The unspoken end to the sentence made her pulse punch erratically because, of course, they were on his turf now. Here in Italy, she knew no one. She couldn't even speak the language.

Actually, that wasn't quite true, she thought, her face suddenly burning. Ettore had taught her a few very specific words.

Her breath snagged and maybe it was audible because his jaw flexed and she felt a shiver scrabble over her skin and then, to hide her reaction, she said quickly, 'How far is it to your house?'

He hesitated a moment, and she had the feeling that

he was debating something. 'Just over an hour,' he said finally.

'And when are we going to see your father?'

'He'll be there when we arrive. He lives with me.'

He did? How was that going to work?

The panic she had been largely keeping at bay since she'd boarded her flight in London surged up inside her as the private time she would need to survive this arrangement they'd made seemed to evaporate before her eyes.

'You don't need to worry. He has his own rooms. But he rarely gets up before lunch, and he usually retires early.'

'How did he react when you told him about the marriage?'

'He was surprised, obviously. But he's looking forward to meeting you.'

Dulcie tried to imagine her own father's reaction. Colin Turner had been a controlling husband and a controlling father. That choice he had forced her to make as a child had been the first of many. She'd learned which path to follow to earn his approval, and he'd had her whole life mapped out.

Obedience had been rewarded but any deviation from the path he'd chosen had resulted in coldness and distance. After she'd changed her degree course from law to environmental sciences, he had stopped paying her tuition fees and her living expenses.

When, finally, she had learned the extent of his control and cruelty, she had chosen to walk away, and he had punished her by cutting her out of his life.

'Do you want to start or shall I?'

She glanced over at Ettore. 'Start what?'

'We need to fill in the gaps. In our lives. It's what we'd do if this reconciliation were real.'

'You know what I do. I work at the lab as a technician and then I do shifts as a cleaner at the university.'

She knew she sounded like some truculent teenager, but when she'd met Ettore, she'd still been riding high from being offered her dream job at Genesis Agri-Tech. It was humbling to have to relive her bumpy descent down the ladder.

'I'm not talking about the broad brushstrokes. We need to dig deeper. Get into the finer details. Like what you do outside work.'

There was nothing outside work. Her school and university friends kept in touch, but it was hard to do more than text them and meet for an occasional quick catch-up. And since Oscar had moved in with her, he was her focus.

'I see friends. We go out to dinner. We go dancing. We go to parties,' she lied. 'What about you? What have you been up to?'

'I oversee the family business. We own a vineyard. A couple of years ago, we expanded into olive oil.'

How had she not known that? But they had talked about their lives only in terms of the here and now. Everything else had been extraneous. An unwarranted intrusion into something that had felt distant and unconnected to who they were when they were together.

'And outside of growing vines and olives?'

His eyes narrowed on her face. 'I see friends. We go out to dinner, go dancing.'

There was a hard pause.

So much for filling in the gaps. Was this why their

marriage had failed? But why would this version work any better?

Her fingers clenched and unclenched in her lap. She was starting to feel panicky again.

Back in Cambridge, the reality of what she had agreed to do had felt distant and unreal. It had been something happening in a far-off place called the future. It had been easier to focus on her motivation for agreeing. But now that she was here the inherent, unchangeable flaws of the deal they'd made were getting more pertinent by the mile.

'What are they?' Her eyes snagged on a honey-coloured building with crumbling, crenellated walls. Through the gaps she could see some chickens pecking furiously. 'I must have seen five or six already. They look like little fortresses.'

'It's a *masseria.* They're not fortresses so much as fortified houses. They're very common in this region.'

'Sounds welcoming.'

His mouth curved up minutely at the corners and she knew that he knew that she was referring to that remark he had made in Cambridge, and she had to fight back a betraying sort of flush at the idea that they should be in any way on the same wavelength.

'Six hundred years ago there used to be pirates along the coast, and I suppose the residents got fed up with being raided and robbed so the landowners built these fortified houses.'

'Why didn't they just build castles?'

'Some of them did.' He lifted his hand from the wheel and gestured to his left and her gaze followed his gesture.

She sat up sharply, her eyes widening.

Even at a distance she could see the turrets of what was unmistakably a castle, half hidden by woodland.

And then it disappeared from view.

Turning in her seat, she peered past the headrest trying to see it again. And then she froze.

Ettore glanced at her. 'What is it?'

'Those SUVs were at the airport. I think we're being followed.'

'Yes, we are,' he said calmly. 'It's their job, and, unfortunately, they're something you'll have to come to terms with.'

'What do you mean?' She frowned, and now it was her turn to look over at him.

'It comes with the territory,' he said as he accelerated through a pair of huge wrought-iron gates that opened silently to let them pass. 'Or rather it comes with the estate.'

'What are you talking about? What estate?'

A shiver ran down her spine, a child again playing Grandmother's Footsteps, feeling something creeping up behind her, something she didn't want to turn and face. But this time Ettore was giving her no choices.

He shifted back in his seat, his dark gold gaze tearing into her.

'This is Castiglione Fiana, and it is my family's home. Which means, as of now, it is your home too.'

Her breath, her heartbeat, everything fell still. This was his family home?

But what kind of family lived in a castle? In England, they would have to be ultra wealthy or, more likely, aristocratic.

She thought back to the beautiful, serious-eyed man she had met in Paris, remembering how formal he could sometimes be with strangers and that slight aloofness of manner that seemed to magically conjure up a seat in a crowded restaurant. And then her hands started to tremble and there was a ringing in her ears, and she understood it all in that instant and it was as crushing as it was overwhelming. Because the clues had always been there but she'd been too busy hiding herself to see what was hiding in plain sight.

'Who are your family?'

He hesitated infinitesimally as if the question was something he'd fielded many times already in his life.

'My father is the Duke of Marchesi. I am his heir, the Marquis of Corti.'

For a moment, the interior of the car seemed to flex in on itself as if all the air had been sucked out if it. They had stopped moving but Dulcie barely noticed. Nor did she register the moment when Ettore got out of the car. It was only when he opened her door and held out his hand and then, moments later, attempted to take hers, that her body reacted and she pulled her hand back.

For a moment, his smile looked as if it were stamped onto his face, and she suddenly noticed that they were no longer alone. There were two people, a man and a woman, standing in front of the largest door she had ever seen. His family? No, they must be staff, she realised a moment later as the woman stepped forward, inclining her head, her knees dipping into what looked suspiciously like a curtsey.

'Buongiorno, Signore, Signora.'

'*Buongiorno*, Valentina. *Cara*, this is Valentina, our housekeeper. And that is Alberto.' The man bowed stiffly.

'Hi, nice to meet you both.' Dulcie forced herself to

smile, and this time when Ettore took her hand, she managed not to jerk away.

Ignoring the sparks shooting up her arm, she let him lead her into the castle.

'I'll give you the guided tour tomorrow, but I'm sure you'll want to see your room and relax after the journey,' Ettore said smoothly. Without pausing, he turned towards Valentina and started speaking in rapid Italian. The housekeeper nodded, inclined her head, and then once again they were alone.

'Here we are.'

Ettore strode through a doorway, and Dulcie followed him and stopped, panic pinwheeling inside her ribcage.

She spun wordlessly in a circle, her gaze absorbing the grandeur of her surroundings, although it was hard to take it in. Cambridge was old, maybe older than this in places, and some of the buildings, like King's College, were not just old but iconic. But they were public buildings.

This was Ettore's home. Her home too and she felt her fury and some other shivering emotion snatch at her breath.

Refusing to meet his gaze, she stared across the room. She had grown up in comfort, but this was pure, undiluted opulence. The ceilings were high and vaulted, and decorated with what could only be described as a work of art. She gazed upwards at the fresco, her head still swimming, trying to imagine how, when, who had painted it.

Following her gaze, Ettore said matter-of-factly, 'It's believed to have been painted in late 1500s. My family would like it to be by Caravaggio, but it's been authenticated and it's not.'

He lifted a shoulder in an almost imperceptible shrug,

and now she could see it in his movements, the heir to a dukedom, an aristocrat mourning the lowly provenance of his fresco.

'On the plus side, most of it is original but some areas were damaged during the Second World War. Not intentionally. It was a stray bomb that was intended for the ports, but the castle took a hit and some of the building sustained structural and architectural damage. It's only recently been restored.'

She stared at the ceiling, trying to see the difference, but she was a scientist by nature and instead she let her eyes drift over the huge four-poster bed and a dressing table fit for a princess. Someone, possibly Valentina, had placed a probably priceless vase of pale pink peonies on a small low table and, gazing at their delicate, splaying petals, she felt slightly sick.

There was another door and Ettore gestured towards it negligently.

'Through there is your bathroom and dressing room.'

As her eyes jerked to his, he flicked on the light. 'As my father's health has deteriorated, I have taken on most of his social engagements. Obviously, you will have to accompany me to some of those events, so I had Valentina speak to a stylist and she sent over some suitable clothes and shoes.'

Her eyes moved over the rail of shimmering silk evening gowns and lightweight, candy-coloured day dresses. 'How did you know my size?'

'You're my wife. Some things, once known, are never forgotten,' he said obliquely. 'If you don't like them or they don't fit, then tell Valentina and she will arrange for replacements.'

Really? Was that what he thought was her most pressing concern here? She stared at him, a wave of anger rising inside her, tangled up with a hurt that she refused to acknowledge in Ettore's presence. Clearly, she succeeded because after a moment he switched off the light and said, 'It's a lot to process, I know, but you've adapted to worse.'

The arrogance and lack of empathy in his words made her want to snatch up the vase of peonies and bring it crashing down on his head.

Instead, she said coolly, 'How long exactly have you lived here?'

'Since I was born.'

'And you didn't think to tell me that before.' She thought back to when she'd asked him about his house in the car, and he'd hesitated.

'I did consider telling you at the airport, but I thought it was something that would be better understood in person.'

'I don't mean now. I mean, why didn't you tell me two years ago?' But even before he answered she knew that he had kept that part of himself separate and secret because, despite marrying her, he had never committed to the idea of her being here with him, for real.

'It didn't come up. Like your brother didn't come up.'

She felt her spine stiffen. 'You met him, remember?'

'It's not something I'm ever likely to forget.'

His face was interchangeable with the stone of the walls and the cold distance in his voice made her want to crawl under the huge bed. But now at least she understood why he had been so appalled by Oscar's drunken antics.

'That makes two of us,' she said.

His dark gold eyes burned into her. 'It's probably best

if we avoid discussing certain aspects of our past. I am prepared to put them behind us, you should too.'

She stared at him in silent disbelief. 'You know, it astonishes me that I ever considered marrying you without any financial incentive.'

They were back to square one.

He sighed. 'Let's concentrate on the present, shall we?'

'Yes, let's.' She squared her shoulders. 'So in the present, where do you sleep?'

'My room is through that door.' He gestured to a third, closed door.

'Which I hope is locked.'

His eyes glittered in a way that made something curl inside her. 'You clearly don't know me very well if you think I'm the kind of man who forces himself on women.'

'Oh, I don't know you well at all, Ettore. But I do know that you're the kind of man who manipulates women.'

'One woman. You. And you could have refused me. Which says as much about you as it does me. Because I know you, Dulcie. I know your price. But be very clear, you are going to earn it. My father needs to believe in us. If we're going to pass as a happily married couple who have seized a second chance at love, you can't be like this. We won't get away with it. We need to feel connected. Close. Which means no more jerking away from me if I ask you to pass the salt at lunch. Or try and hold your hand.

'Because, in case it's slipped your mind, at some point we are going to have to kiss, so perhaps you should start getting your head round that now. In fact, might I suggest you get in a bit of practice?' His eyes snaked from her face to her clenched fist.

'Although you might want to adjust the position of your thumb. Unless, of course, you'd like me to help in person.'

As she watched the door close behind him, she felt her cheeks grow warm. One night, in bed, she had admitted to Ettore that, before she'd got a boyfriend, she had practised kissing by making an O shape with her thumb and forefinger.

Only now it appeared she had been telling her secrets to a stranger. Was this the real Ettore? Maybe. But then this wasn't a real marriage.

She felt suddenly furious with herself but mostly with Ettore. It had taken her every single day of the last two years to get her life back on track and in that entire time he hadn't so much as texted.

But when he'd needed something from her, he had simply turned up on her doorstep, or as good as, offering her that wrecking ball of a choice.

Come to Italy as his wife or refuse and knowingly turn down money that could help Oscar turn his life around.

She hated that it was all so easy for him. That he could just ambush her like that and cold-bloodedly use their marriage as a bargaining chip. But most of all she hated that this was her life now and for the foreseeable future.

CHAPTER FIVE

'So, Dulcie. Let me look at you.' Edoardo Marchesi smiled. 'I see that your name is entirely appropriate. It is beautiful, and you are a very beautiful woman.'

Ettore watched in silence as his father leaned forward to gaze deeply into Dulcie's eyes. 'It comes from the Latin word "dulce", meaning sweet.'

Despite having an oxygen canister placed near his wheelchair that sat discreetly at the edge of the room, the old man was an incurable flirt.

Women liked him, they always had. He was handsome and very masculine without being lecherous or toxic. Which no doubt explained why he'd had so many affairs.

And he liked women. He liked their company. He liked hearing them laugh. Liked making them laugh. Even now, in his eighties, he had what Sofia called 'riz'. Charisma and charm and, unlike other men his age and younger, he was not having plastic surgery or hair transplants. On the contrary, he had turned ageing into an act of elegance.

'Ettore told me that when we first met, didn't you, darling?'

He felt his body tense as Dulcie glanced across the table and smiled at him, one of those lush smiles that were as rare and warming as winter sunlight. In the past, he had been a collector of such smiles in the same way that his great-great-grandfather had once collected fine art from around the globe.

And superficially, certainly to his father and the staff who were hovering discreetly at the margins of the room, it looked real, as if all those weeks and months and years of silent impasse were not a vast, invisible and unassailable chasm between them.

'I did.'

Ettore shifted minutely in his seat so that he could better meet Dulcie's teasing gaze. Back then, it wasn't just her smiles he'd collected. He had studied her greedily as any student in love with his subject would pore over his books. In the past, he had been attuned to her body, to her breath, to the slightest tilt of her chin and he could see from the slight creasing around her eyes that she was faking it.

Of course she was faking it, he thought irritably. That was the set-up. It was hypocritical of him to mind, and yet he found that he did. Minded more that she was making it look so effortless because, despite expectations to the contrary, he was finding it harder than he'd thought.

His jaw tightened. He should just be pleased that Dulcie was doing what he'd asked her to do. *Told* her to do. *Threatened* her into doing?

The vice around his chest ratcheted up a notch.

Had he threatened her? Not explicitly. But there had been a threat implied, of consequences that would follow if his conditions weren't met.

It was a not too-distant relation of the assumptions that his uncle and cousins employed so frequently, which he claimed to despise. But Dulcie had made him a stranger to himself before. Why should today be any different?

He felt his father's gaze graze his face.

'Ettore was the scholar of the family. He got full marks in his *maturità*. His sister, Sofia, is the creative thinker, but Ettore always saw the bigger picture. Even as a child, he understood what needed to be done and he would make it happen too.'

'I can believe that.' Dulcie's voice was pitch perfect. In fact, her whole performance was perfect. There were those smiles, warm, open, not fawning, but engaged and receptive. And she had leaned into Ettore's body as he'd introduced her to his father.

Introducing her to his father was always going to be the most hazardous moment of the lunch but intuitively she had understood that there was no need for some lengthy, public explanation for their past estrangement or their recent reconciliation. A marriage was a private matter between husband and wife. Instead, she had focused on the present.

No wonder his father was so captivated. Ignoring the unpalatable and diverting attention away to something new and shiny was practically a mandate for the aristocracy. It had certainly enabled their survival. Although his family appeared to have missed that memo. Mostly they preferred that other aristocratic standby. Do as I say, not as I do.

'And what about you, my dear? Are you an academic too?'

'I'm in the process of completing my MSc in plant sciences, specialising in sustainable agriculture.'

Was she? Ettore felt her admission as a tiny twist to his

stomach. He knew she was completing a master's, but the list of bullet points she'd emailed him hadn't hinted at the pride and passion weaving through her voice.

'I'm afraid that is something we're not used to as a family. Brains as well as beauty. Mostly we have one or the other so you will be a rare and welcome addition.'

Edoardo's easy smile tightened, and he tensed, his hand slithering down the stem of his wine glass, which tilted ominously to one side.

'Papà—' Ettore was on his feet, reaching across the table, but Dulcie was quicker.

'Here, let me.' She deftly righted the glass, her mouth curving into a gentle smile that reached her eyes and softened her face, and Ettore tried not to feel mean-spirited. Because that smile, he would take. But Dulcie wasn't directing it at him, but his father.

'Are you okay, Papà? Should I—?'

'I don't need anyone fussing over me. *Giancarlo.*' The old man raised his hand imperiously and a young man wearing chinos and a polo shirt appeared like a genie summoned by some invisible lamp. 'I should like to return to my room now. It is a delight to meet you, my dear. Giancarlo, give me your arm.'

There was a silence as the two men walked towards the door. Edoardo's gait was steady, his spine upright, but Ettore knew his father would lean more heavily onto the younger man's arm as soon as they were out of sight.

'We'll take coffee on the terrace, please, Valentina.' Ettore got to his feet, somewhat imperiously, and to his surprise Dulcie did too. But only, no doubt, because being outside felt less intimate, he thought as she followed him onto the paved terrace. He gestured towards the chairs that were set out under the shade of a palm tree, and she sat down, curling her legs under her chair, every inch the duchess-in-waiting.

Glancing up, she frowned at the palms. 'These aren't native to this region, are they?'

Ettore shook his head. 'My great-great-grandfather had them imported. They were something of a status symbol at the time.'

One delicate eyebrow arched.

'I didn't know aristocrats did that whole keeping-up-with-the Joneses thing.'

'Here, it would be more a case of keeping up with the Rossis, and aristocrats, even those whose titles are merely honorifics, are not immune to one-upmanship. On the contrary, it's their life blood.'

They fell silent as Valentina arrived with coffee and a tray of petits fours and, as she retreated, Dulcie seemed lost in thought.

'Do you still drink your coffee with milk?'

She nodded, her eyes still fixed on the palm, and then she said quietly, 'How ill is he?'

It was a perfectly reasonable question, but hearing Dulcie ask it was unbalancing in a way that he couldn't explain.

'It's difficult to say,' he said as her eyes moved to his face. 'He refuses to talk about it with me. And as you can see, he's frail but he's all there mentally so, short of hacking his medical records, I don't have the full facts.'

She bit her lip, glanced away towards the dark verdant woods that curled in a wide semicircle around the entire estate.

'I know we're doing it for the right reasons, but I don't like lying to him. It feels wrong. It is wrong.'

He felt a prickle of resentment. Did she think this was easy for him? That his life had been easy because he lived in a castle? He was doing this for his family. To protect the legacy of six hundred years of history. Because unlike his family, unlike the majority of people, he understood Castiglione Fiana's true value lay not in its status but its steadfastness.

But explaining that to Dulcie would mean unravelling his all too recent history and, in doing so, he would reveal too much about the family she had married into, and his place in it. And what would be the point? She couldn't understand. Unconditional love was clearly a cornerstone of her family life. Just look at how fiercely protective she was of Oscar.

He had a sharp, stinging flashback to Dulcie catching fire, the shake in her voice as she picked her brother over him, and the tension he'd been carrying for weeks now found a focus.

'I'm sure you'll get over it. Doing the wrong thing comes so naturally to you.'

A second after he spoke, even before he saw thc stunned, uncomprehending look on her face, he regretted his words.

'Would you like anything else, Signore?'

He swore silently. Valentina was back. He watched as Dulcie looked up at her and smiled.

'Not for me, *grazie*, Valentina. All this beautiful sunshine has made me feel a little sleepy. I'm going to have a lie-down.'

As she pushed back her chair, he got to his feet, and

she held his gaze for a full sixty seconds and then she held out her hand.

After another sixty seconds, he took it. It was like holding a piece of wood.

He followed her into her bedroom, closing the door behind them.

'Dulcie—'

'I really am quite tired.' Her voice was wooden too, as if she were a bad actor speaking bad dialogue in a play he had written, and, not liking how that made him feel, he walked over to the adjoining door between their two rooms and made his own voice brisk.

'Knock when you get up and I'll come through and we can go down together.'

She nodded, and that mechanical nod was the last thing he saw before she closed the door in his face. Seconds later, he heard the key turn in the lock, and he turned and walked slowly over to the bed. He had spent most of his life feeling boxed in and contained by the personalities around him, defined by their dislikes and preferences. But now, even though he was locked out, not locked in, he had never felt more trapped.

His gaze moved slowly around his room. He loved the castle, knew that living there was a privilege. But he had never wanted to run the estate or be the heir apparent. Or become the caretaker-cum-manager of his entire family.

It had happened by osmosis. It didn't matter that for most of his life somebody else had been technically in charge. His great-grandfather. Then his grandfather. His father. And, briefly, Edo, his charming older brother who was adored not just by his mother but by the very people who had lost their jobs in the redundancies Ettore had had to implement to pay back Edo's debts.

Of course, nobody knew that. Just as nobody knew that it was he who had sat down with his father and convinced him that the only way to save the estate from the mess his grandfather left behind was to sell off the other properties that his forebears had amassed over six hundred years.

He hadn't wanted to make those decisions. And yet, someone had had to make them. That someone should have been Edo.

But the wrong brother had died.

That was what his mother had thought. And said to him after Edo's death.

He knew she'd been grief-stricken, raging against a world that had robbed her of her child. But he was her child too.

Her second son, the middle child, the spare, although truthfully, he hadn't even been that. That would imply he could replace his brother and that simply wasn't true. He'd known that for what felt like for ever, just as he'd known that his father doted on Sofia. His was the hand that had always got held by the nanny.

His body tensed against the horsehair and pocket-sprung mattress as he heard the creak of the French windows being pushed open next door.

Dulcie.

Getting to his feet, he walked towards his own closed windows, drawn to an image of her standing on her balcony like some modern-day Juliet—

He froze, his eyes narrowing incredulously through the glass, hardly able to believe what he was seeing as Dulcie twisted her body over the balustrade and began climbing down the twisted, woody trunk of the wisteria that clung to the stone outside her room.

She slithered down the last few feet and dropped to the ground. Then she wiped her hands on her dress, slipped her shoes back on her feet and started walking purposefully towards the gardens.

It was a surprisingly easy climb, Dulcie thought. As her feet touched the warm terrace, she felt grounded, metaphorically and literally.

Slipping her shoes back on, she headed towards the formal gardens. But they weren't what interested her. And, walking swiftly, she made her way between the mathematically straight box hedges to what lay on the other side of a sun-soaked brick wall.

She hadn't been lying to Valentina, she did feel exhausted physically and emotionally, but she was hardly going to fall asleep with that snarky comment Ettore had made about honesty replaying inside her head. As if he hadn't just revealed to her hours earlier that he was a marquis who lived in this castle.

The hypocrisy of it stung almost as much as the judgement in his eyes.

She squared her shoulders. Then why was she letting him get inside her head? He might be her husband, but she wasn't some method actress immersing herself in her role. Right now, she was just Dulcie.

Feeling calmer, she pulled open the heavy oak door and stepped through it into—

She sucked in a breath, stunned, speechless.

The vineyard stretched out in every direction. There were no grapes, but the gnarled canes of the vines were covered in tender shoots and delicate, lobed leaves of every possible shade of green from a pale eau de Nil to a deeper, richer emerald.

Transfixed, she walked down the first row, her fingers grazing the soft, veined leaves. They weren't just green. Some of the younger shoots had a reddish, purplish tinge. She frowned. Up close, she could see some were damaged. They were flecked with brown spots and torn in places.

'You know, if you keep on disobeying me every time I ask you to do something, this is going to be a very challenging experience for the both of us.'

She spun round, blinking into the sunlight, temporarily blinded. But she didn't need to see the man's face to know who had spoken. She would know his voice in the dark. In fact, if Ettore hadn't spoken at all, and she were blindfolded, she would know it was him because her heart, which had been beating out a slow, steady drum roll of appreciation, was now pounding out of time.

'It already is.' Tilting up her chin, instantly bracing for battle, she lifted her hand to block out the sun's ray and Ettore's face slid into focus.

'You were supposed to knock on my door when you woke up. Not climb out of the window.' His expression was impossible to read but there was a mildness to his voice that defused some of her fire.

'I thought you were sleeping. And I know we're supposed to be unhinged with love but people in love can spend some time apart. They don't have to be joined at the hip.'

His eyes moved over her face like a caress. 'Where would you like to be joined?'

Her breath snapped tight in her chest, skin flushing hot as she remembered his mouth on hers.

Clearing her throat, she shrugged. 'I just needed some space.'

'You want a larger room?'

She sighed. 'Not that kind of space.'

The sun appeared from behind a cloud, and she took the opportunity to transfer her attention back to the vines.

'How long ago did you have a hailstorm?'

She sensed his surprise. 'Three weeks.'

'You don't have hail nets.'

He took a step closer, and now she could see that he was shaking his head. 'The last big hailstorm to hit this region was probably two years ago so it doesn't make economic sense. But if they keep increasing, then, perhaps, I will have to consider it.'

I, not we. She remembered the moment after lunch when he had said that aristocrats were not immune to wanting to keep up appearances. That it was their lifeblood. *Theirs*, not mine. But he was an aristocrat too. And wasn't this a family business? Was it simply a slip of the tongue?

Not that it mattered.

This relationship was transactional for both of them. Their reacquainted status didn't require her to know or genuinely care about the answers to those questions. Better to focus on something neutral like climate issues.

'So, you have problems with—'

'Would you like to—?'

They both spoke at once.

'You first.' She smiled stiffly.

'I was just going to ask if you'd like to take a look around the estate.'

His gaze tracked across the vines to where an ATV was trundling towards them. She felt her heart leap with relief. A tour of the estate would be a welcome distraction.

'I'd love that,' she said, and for the first time since she had arrived in Italy her enthusiasm was genuine.

'Good.' He seemed pleased. 'It's too far to walk, particularly in those shoes. But if we take one of the ATVs it should be fine.'

We, not you.

Her momentary relief faltered. She'd assumed one of Ettore's farmhands would take her. But now it appeared that he was planning on going with her.

'Don't feel like you have to change your plans. I don't want to take up your time.'

His gaze travelled over her face, seeing too much, no doubt seeing the mistake she had made and the conflict she was now feeling.

'My time is your time. And besides, I can't think of a more enjoyable way to spend an afternoon than showing my wife around her new home. Particularly if it stops her from climbing out of her window and startling my staff.'

A group of estate workers appeared then, stopping to nod deferentially at their boss and the boss's wife, and, after a moment of silent frustration at having once again been the agent of her own downfall, she followed him numbly to a stone barn. Like all the buildings on the estate, it was old, but unlike the barns she had seen on the drive over, the walls weren't crumbling and inside the floor was swept, and several ATVs were parked in a neat line.

'You'll need one of these.' He picked up a helmet and handed it to her, then frowned. 'Given the time of day, it might be quicker to cut through the woods, so I think we'll use the dirt bikes.'

She was shaking her head. 'But I don't know how to ride a bike.'

'That's okay. You can ride pillion. Like you did in Paris. Or have you forgotten about Paris?' he added after a tense, electric moment she didn't fully understand but felt everywhere anyway.

Paris.

It was the first time that either of them had acknowledged those two weeks. When they had finally emerged from Ettore's hotel room, the storm had long gone. The city had felt newly born in the pale sunshine that had greeted them, and Ettore had suggested they hire scooters.

How could she have resisted?

What woman wouldn't have wanted to ride around the city of love, with her arms wrapped around his waist, his heartbeat beating against her ribs, his blood pulsing in time to hers? She had felt both safe and so intensely happy that she had wept when they had had to hand the scooters back.

Now he held out the helmet as if it were a gauntlet. Which it was, she thought, as something gleamed in his eyes that made heat dance over her skin.

Ten minutes later, she was moving through the lines of vines, her hands tight around the bike's grab rail, her gaze averted from Ettore's broad back, but it was hard not to watch the flex of his glorious muscles as he changed gears or leaned into a turn.

And then they were at the top of a hill, surrounded

by land in every direction, stretching as far as the eye could see.

Ettore stopped the bike and they dismounted. 'This is it. This is our land. My grandfather used to say, "If you can see it, we own it."'

'Is that the sea?' she asked, pointing to a distant blurred blue between the land and the sky, more to hide her stunned reaction than because she cared.

'It's closer than it looks. Hence the pirates I mentioned in the car.'

Her gaze pulled down to a field of trees with pale green leaves. They were silvery with age, and they had an almost architectural stateliness, like tiny cathedrals.

'I thought you'd only just started growing olives. Those look old to me.'

'They are. Some are hundreds of years old. But until a few years ago, we only picked and pressed them for ourselves. But then small-batch estate oils became a thing, so we started selling commercially. We average about three hundred bottles a year. Aside from that they help the biodiversity of the vineyard.'

'Is that why you grow almonds too?'

He nodded. 'In the past, our estate managers were always wedded to fertilisers and chemicals and my forebears were wedded to maximising profit over the environment. But for the last fifty years, the yield has been dropping incrementally. So about five years ago, I started to look at sustainable viticulture. My aim has been to promote a healthy ecosystem rooted in more historical traditions like *vite maritata*, training vines to grow on living trees.'

Dulcie nodded. 'Is it just olives and almonds?'

'No, we have maples, cherry, plum, fig—'

'How is that working?'

His face softened a fraction and a tension she hadn't realised he was holding in his shoulders seemed to lift a little.

'It's been a challenge. During the transition from chemicals, we took a hit financially, but since then it's been on an upward trajectory in terms of yield and last year we had our best year ever.'

She could believe it. There was a promise of abundance, the potential for a bountiful harvest everywhere she looked. And a sense of nurturing and meticulous care, of human intervention but in harmony with nature.

All of it apparently down to Ettore.

It was strange and a little sad to think that they had been husband and wife and yet she had known nothing about any of this. How had that happened? But she had never pushed him to talk about his life before her, because that would have meant talking about her home life, her past, herself and, of course, the decision she'd made to abandon her brother. And if she couldn't forgive herself for what she had done to Oscar, how could she expect anyone else to?

It was why everything they'd 'shared' had been superficial.

Except in bed. That was when, how, they had communicated deeply. But why get married, then? Why hadn't they just stayed in bed until the fire that blazed between them had burned out?

A shrill, repetitive ringing sound punctuated that thought and Ettore fished out his phone. Glancing at the screen, he frowned. 'I need to take this.'

'Go ahead.' She gave him a small, stiff smile. 'I can entertain myself.'

As Ettore answered his phone, she walked back over to where the bike was parked. She swung her leg over the seat, and sat down, letting her gaze drift across the landscape. It was a paradise. And finally, and without any kind of strange, artificial intervention, she and Ettore had found a common ground.

If only she didn't have to lie to Edoardo.

Her fingers tightened around the bike handles, and she felt a sudden urge to flee the scene of the crime. Except she didn't know how to ride the bike. Or perhaps she did. How hard could it be?

Tentatively, she turned the key as Ettore had done, then flicked the engine on switch. Now, just a little bit of throttle. She turned the handlebar—

There was a roar, much louder than she'd anticipated. Startled, she let go of the handlebars as the bike jerked forward, rearing up like a startled horse, and then she was falling backwards, her breath punching out of her mouth audibly as she sat down heavily on the ground.

The bike was still moving, speeding forward down the slope and then there was the sound of wood splintering and fibreglass cracking as it collided with a fence post and slid sideways, its wheels spinning in the air.

'Ma che cazzo fai?'

Ettore was by her side, leaning over her, his face in shadow, his eyes moving over her anxiously and she didn't need to speak Italian to know that he was swearing.

'What are you playing at?'

'Nothing. I was—' It was too complicated to explain.

'Are you hurt?'

'No.' Bruised maybe, but mostly that was just her pride, she thought, watching his face harden as she shook her head.

'Wait here.'

He got to his feet and stalked down the hill to where the bike lay on its side beneath a fence post, wire tangled around the chassis. It took a moment or two of twisting and tugging, but he managed to pull it free and lift it upright.

'Is it okay?'

'It's fine,' he said tersely, and the easy mood between them was a distant memory now. 'We should get back. Are you okay to ride?'

'Yes, of course.'

He stared at her for a moment as if debating whether or not to believe her and then he handed her a helmet.

Her coccyx was already starting to feel sore by the time they reached the barn. Ettore spoke to a man wearing overalls about the bike and then he took her hand and practically frogmarched her back to the castle.

'I have a couple of calls to make. Dinner is at eight. We'll eat on the terrace. What? What is it?' He was staring at her face, frowning.

'You're hurt—'

She stared anxiously at where blood was seeping through the fabric of his shirt.

He glanced down, frowned.

'Oh, that, I caught it on the wire when I was pulling the bike free.'

'Let me see.' She reached out.

'No.'

Her chin jerked up as his hand clamped around hers.

'I can manage. There's no one watching, you don't need to pretend you care.'

She flinched. 'I'm not pretending. I just wanted to—'

His beautiful mouth was set in a taut line, and there was a knife-edged tension to his body now. 'And I just want you to go to your room and try not to do anything reckless or stupid.'

There was a pulsing silence. She stared at him, frozen with shock and misery.

'Given that I agreed to come here as your wife, I'd say it's way too late for that,' she said slowly, and she turned and walked up the stairs and into her room.

CHAPTER SIX

ETTORE LIFTED HIS glass of perfectly chilled Prosecco, savouring the first kiss of tiny bubbles. Personally, he preferred the Verdeca produced on the estate. But Prosecco was arguably the star of Italian wine exports, beloved of people all over the world who were looking to celebrate or commemorate or commiserate.

His eyes tracked across the terrace, moving between his relations. He wondered what they were here to do today. Obviously, typically, a meal to meet a new addition to the family would be a cause of celebration.

But his family was not like other families.

Ever since his grandfather's death, and his own father's elevation to the status of Duke, his uncle and his cousins had been circling at the sidelines. They were tempered somewhat in the presence of Edoardo, but they shared a sense of aggrievement at having missed out on the top prize. Not that it stopped any of them living their lives exactly as they pleased whatever the cost or the consequences.

And they all loved a party.

Ettore glanced over at where his father was talking to his sister-in-law and sipping a glass of Prosecco. He wasn't meant to be drinking, but then neither should he be hosting a party. But that hadn't stopped Edoardo from issuing a last-minute dinner invitation to his entire extended family to meet Dulcie.

And here they all were. Ettore's uncle Frederico, his aunt Constanza, his cousins, Francesco, Giorgio and Beppe, together with the current iteration of interchangeable model or wannabe actress girlfriends who his cousins chewed up and spat out on a bi-monthly basis.

Francesco, his uncle Frederico's oldest son, older, in fact, than him by three weeks, was gazing lazily across the terrace, glass in hand, but he could sense his cousin's curiosity. It was why Francesco was there. Why all his relations were there. Aside from himself, a short attention span was a family trait. They were like babies. They liked the novel and the random. And nothing could be more random than Ettore turning up with a wife out of the blue.

'I have to say, you're full of surprises, *fra*.'

His cousin's mouth pulled into a shape that was somewhere between a jeer and a pout. 'I mean, a wife.' He puffed up his cheeks and blew them out, mimicking an explosion.

'It's not that surprising, Checco.'

'So where is she, then? Your English rose.' He made a small, mocking bow. 'My bad, I meant La Marchesa?'

Ettore felt his spine stiffen infinitesimally. The answer to that question, or rather its un-answerability, made his pulse thrum through his limbs as if he were prepping for a race. Or a fight.

Another fight, he thought, and he had to stop himself from striding back into the castle and straight into her room to finish the one he'd started yesterday at the bottom of the stairs. Although it would be quite the fight. Dulcie had looked as if she wanted to strangle him.

But she'd had no right to be angry. No understanding of what it had felt like to turn and see the bike rear up and her body fall backwards, to hear that shattering sound of metal hitting wood. Even as he'd run towards her, he'd known, logically, that she shouldn't be badly hurt. But it hadn't stopped his limbs from feeling light and airless. Or his brain from replaying the moment when his brother's bike had flipped over.

Feeling scared, feeling anything, was not supposed to be a part of this arrangement and so he'd lashed out, sought refuge from his panic and fear in anger. And he had still been angry when she'd noticed he was bleeding.

Glancing down at his shirt, he could see the faint outline of the plaster covering the wound on his stomach. It wasn't quite the scratch he'd made it out to be. The wire had snagged on his skin and punctured it as he'd wrenched the bike free.

But he wasn't the only one hurting.

He'd been brusque with her. Too brusque.

And now she was punishing him.

She had joined him for dinner last night. Smiled, laughed, touched his arm, looked into his eyes. It was her best ever performance. Anyone watching would have thought she was so in love with him that she could hardly see straight.

And then they had gone upstairs, and as he'd closed her bedroom door, it was as if a switch had flipped. The smile had faded and her voice had flattened as she'd said goodnight.

At breakfast, she had turned back into a smiling, nodding doll. Lunch had been a near identical performance. And it was driving him insane. Only he could hardly demand that she be herself, could he?

His groin hardened as he remembered that kiss in his hotel room and how her hand had been pushing and pressing against his chest as if she hadn't been sure what she'd wanted to happen. But her mouth had been sure.

Right now, though, he wasn't entirely sure that Dulcie would even show up.

Pushing that thought away, he smiled at his cousin. 'She's just getting ready.'

Or shinning down the ivy again, only this time with her suitcase in tow.

'Apparently she is ready,' Checco said, and Ettore felt his cousin, felt the entire gathering, shift direction minutely. The flow of conversation receded like a wave pulling away from the shoreline and the terrace seemed to shrink inwards, centring on the woman in the simple V-neck, sleeveless dress.

Ettore felt his throat constrict. He never tired of looking at the castle or the land around it. Every day he marvelled at the majesty and beauty of his surroundings. But Dulcie was so beautiful she made all of it disappear.

His gaze moved hungrily over the cornflower-blue floral fabric that clung to her breasts and waist before flaring out to a skirt that skimmed her mid thighs.

The stylist had chosen well, but Dulcie wore it better. The dress had a hint of sixties flowerchild that matched the challenge in her blue eyes. It was what had first attracted him to her. The women he knew, the women he'd dated before her, were like hothouse orchids, trained from birth to aspire to perfection.

Dulcie was more like the wildflowers that breached the estate's stone walls and pushed up through the earth to cluster around the base of the vines. Nothing would ever keep her down for long, he thought with relief. She would always push back, fight for the light.

He heard Checco whistle softly between his teeth, but he was already moving towards her.

As he stopped beside her, he hesitated then leaned in and kissed her softly on the mouth. 'You look beautiful.'

'Thank you. Sorry, I'm late,' she murmured, her voice just loud enough for those nearby to hear. 'I just couldn't get my hair to do what I wanted. Valentina had to help me.'

Her hair was swept up into another updo, this one more elegant than the previous. But a few rebellious curls still framed her face. Despite that, she looked every inch the perfect wife, the perfect marchesa.

'Aren't you going to introduce us?' Checco appeared at his elbow; his dark brown eyes were narrowed in approval.

He held out his hand and when Dulcie held out hers, he lifted it to his mouth.

'Sono incantato,' he said softly. 'I'm Francesco, Ettore's cousin, but everyone calls me Checco.'

'Dulcie. But I guess you know that already.'

'I believe this is your first time to Fiana.' Ettore's uncle stepped forward smoothly.

'Yes, it's beautiful.' Dulcie smiled. 'I feel like I'm dreaming. I keep having to pinch myself.'

'It has that effect, I'm told. Obviously, we're all so used to it.'

Ettore moved to rest his hand lightly around Dulcie's

waist. 'This is my uncle, Frederico. My father's younger brother.'

'Younger but no less deserving.' Frederico smiled languidly. 'We've all been so excited to meet you, Dulcie. I think maybe you have bewitched my nephew. He's always been so critical of our impulsiveness. And yet all along he's had a secret wife.'

'It wasn't a secret, Zio,' Ettore said calmly. He was used to his uncle pushing buttons.

Frederico raised an eyebrow, doing confusion. 'Did I miss the wedding invitation?'

'It was very small. Just the two of us and the witnesses. We didn't want to turn the wedding into a circus.'

'But you did keep it a secret after that.' His uncle persisted. 'For two years. I wonder why that was.'

Beside him, he felt Dulcie stiffen minutely. It was a version of the question Dulcie had asked him in London when she came to his hotel room. His answer was simple. Stick to the truth. Don't elaborate. Only then the mood had shifted. They had talked a little, and in talking, the tension between them had eased, and then…

And then they had kissed.

The memory of her lips on his swelled inside him, and suddenly it was all he could think about. Not just the kiss, but the realness of it and the truth of what happened in his hotel room and before when he and Dulcie had split up. How he had wanted to bury the pain of her rejection.

'It's not that complicated. We split up,' he said quickly. 'It was hard, harder than we both thought it would be, to unpick our lives, and it became an issue between us, and one day we argued, and it got out of hand.'

He had spent most of his life hiding his emotions, his

disappointment, his hurt. But now he let himself sound a little uncomfortable.

'But that doesn't explain why you didn't tell us later.' His uncle frowned, doing confused again. 'I can understand wanting the wedding to be private, but if the marriage was over, why keep it a secret then?'

'Because it wasn't over, and I thought any family involvement, however well intentioned, would only complicate things further. I needed to figure out if we could fix things on our own terms. I was trying to safeguard our chances of reconciliation by keeping it private until we had a clearer path forward.'

Which sounded completely reasonable, except his family would never have tried to fix his marriage. He knew that, more importantly they did, which was no doubt why they were looking at him with the same incredulous expressions on their faces.

There was a beat of silence and then Dulcie said quietly, 'That's not quite what happened.' He felt her turn towards him and, glancing down, he saw that she was looking up at him calmly.

'Ettore is being kind. It was my fault we split up, my fault we didn't get back together sooner. I don't come from this world, and I was nervous about joining it. Ettore wanted to give me time to adjust to the idea of being part of your family. He wasn't being secretive; he was being thoughtful.'

'So, you're saying that you knew who he was all along?' Checco leaned forward, his eyes fixing on Ettore's face, his expression incredulous. 'I thought you hated using your title.'

Dulcie was shaking her head. 'He didn't use it. But he told me about it.'

'If you've finished interrogating my daughter-in-law, Checco…' His father's voice, frail but indomitable.

'I apologise for my family, my dear.' Edoardo lifted his cane, gesturing towards an embossed shield of a rampant lion above the doorway. The same shield that could be found in multiple places around the castle. 'You must feel like you've walked into the lion's den, but I promise—our bark is worse than our bite.'

Now, Dulcie smiled, that same sweet smile that she had bestowed on the old man that first morning at breakfast. 'That's a relief, because I left my chainmail at home.'

The remainder of the evening passed without any further incident. His family seemed to have reluctantly accepted that there was 'nothing to see here' and had typically moved on to talking about themselves.

Eventually, they disappeared one by one until finally it was just Edoardo, Dulcie and himself.

'I have something for you.' The old man reached into his jacket pocket and pulled out a box. 'I want you to have this, Dulcie. It's something I gave to my wife, to Isabella, when she gave birth to Ettore.'

Dulcie felt her eyes burn as Edoardo opened the box and she stared down at a beautiful bracelet set with sapphires and diamonds. It looked old. It looked priceless.

Her hand moved to her throat, to touch the pulse that was beating jerkily against the skin there. 'It's beautiful.'

'It's a Florentine design. Originally acquired by my grandfather for his wife on the birth of their second son.'

She opened her mouth to protest then closed it again.

What was she going to say? *I can't take this because I'm only staying married to your son for money.*

'May I?' The duke loosened the bracelet from the box, and she raised her arm mechanically, and it felt like an out-of-body experience watching him fasten it around her wrist.

Upstairs in her bedroom, Dulcie had almost decided not to come down but then Valentina had knocked on her door and gently offered to help her dress for dinner, and the idea of saying that she wasn't planning on going to the dinner that was being held in her honour had been beyond her.

And it had been nice having Valentina there. Calming and reassuring in the way that she imagined a mother might be.

There were few memories of her mother that could be described as calm. Madeleine Turner was beautiful and before her marriage, she had been a talented artist. But as a mum, she was exhaustingly erratic and emotionally unstable. And subsequent maternal role models had been fleeting. Her father's girlfriends had been kind but remote and, crucially, impermanent. There had been no one to plait her hair or talk to her about her dreams.

Or help her choose what dress to wear to meet her husband's family.

Gazing at her reflection, seeing Valentina smile as she twirled in a circle, Dulcie had felt guilty again for lying. And she wanted to blame Ettore, but the truth was that she had been lying to people in one way or another her whole life.

Sometimes it was a lie of obfuscation. Not lying explicitly but keeping the facts so vague that people naturally came to the wrong conclusion. Other times, it was a lie of omission. She would leave out a salient fact. Like her absent, abandoned brother. And then there were the lies of exaggeration, inflating a truth to shape her story in a way that suited her purpose.

She tried not to think about it. Sometimes, she even imagined telling the truth in all its unvarnished, ugly detail.

Well, not sometimes—once.

Two years ago, she had wanted to tell Ettore the truth about her childhood. Or that was what she told herself. Was that true? She would never know because Oscar's sudden arrival had turned her marriage into a no-man's-land of accusations and lies.

And now there were more lies.

She stared down at the bracelet, her pulse blinking in time to the glittering gemstones as they caught the light.

'I can't take this—'

'You must.' The old man smiled. 'And when your son or daughter has a child of their own, you can pass it on to them. That's what we do. We are only the custodians of all this. The land. The property. This bracelet. We enjoy it and then we pass it on.'

She matched his smile, nodded as if to say, *I understand, I approve.* She could feel Ettore's gaze beating down on her and she tried to pretend that she hadn't noticed and didn't care, but eventually she couldn't help herself and she glanced up to find him watching her intently, his eyes narrowed on her face as if he was trying to read her mind.

'Thank you, Papà. That's very kind of you.'

'It's what your mother would have wanted.'

Had she not been so on edge, so aware of every tiny shift in tension between them, she might not have noticed the subtle change in Ettore's expression.

In Paris, he had given her the briefest details about his family. The email he'd sent her had expanded on those details. She knew that his sister was travelling, his older brother had died in an accident and his mother had also died soon after. But there were no personal stories or insights. And since arriving at the castle, there had been no further revelations. She had seen the family photos in their silver frames clustered on a grand piano but, like all family photos, they concealed as much as they revealed.

Nobody looking at her family photos taken when Oscar was born would have guessed the chaos and conflict behind the smiles. A photo might be worth a thousand words, but they didn't have to be true. In fact, you only really knew what you were looking at if you knew the full story.

And she didn't.

Because, clearly, he was protective of his family and, judging by the almost imperceptible tightening of his mouth when Edoardo mentioned his mother's wishes, he was silently appalled at his father giving something so precious, so laden with meaning, to a woman he was more or less paying to stay as his wife.

Edoardo smiled at her. 'Don't save it for special occasions. I know the insurers would disagree, but beautiful jewels are meant to be worn by beautiful women. Not kept in some vault. Isn't that right, Ettore?'

Ettore didn't speak for a moment but then he nodded stiffly. 'Of course, Papà.'

The old man shifted in his seat. 'Good. And now I

think I need to get some rest. Would you mind if I borrowed your husband for a moment, my dear? I gave Giancarlo the evening off.'

'Of course not.'

Edoardo got to his feet, leaning heavily on his cane. 'Thank you,' she said, and, leaning in, she rose on tiptoe to kiss his papery cheek.

'I'll see you upstairs,' Ettore said quietly.

She waited until the two men had left the terrace and then she turned and walked towards the garden, drawn as ever to the healing calmness of the natural world.

Her eyes dropped to the bracelet. Even without Edoardo's guilt-inducing gift, the evening had been a pretty intimidating encounter. Ettore's family were charming but, despite their languorous manner and drawling voices, his uncle, Frederico, and his cousin, Checco, in particular had picked over her story like Scotland Yard detectives.

Which was why it was so pleasant just to wander across the lawn, stopping occasionally to examine a rose here or a buddleia there. The garden felt like a hybrid to her. Clearly in the past there had been some attempt to impose order but there was also evidence that nature was being allowed to counteract the constraints of the formal garden.

Speaking of constraints…

Glancing down, she slipped off her sandals. Like with the rest of her outfit, she had taken Valentina's advice and gone for a slightly higher heel than she would have chosen for herself, and it wasn't that they were uncomfortable, but, wearing them, she didn't feel like herself, and she had done enough pretending for one day.

The grass felt wonderfully cool beneath her feet. Now, she just needed to let down her hair. Her fingers fumbled against the pins. Usually, she would just use a claw clip, but Valentina had tutted at the thought and deftly pinned her hair into a perfect French twist. Now though, it was hard to know which pin to pull out first.

'Here, let me...'

Her pulse jerked forward as a warm hand touched her neck.

'I can manage,' she protested, but Ettore was already pulling the pins free. She felt her hair come loose, the heavy waves tumbling over her shoulders, and even though she was fully clothed, there was something intimate about a man undoing her hair that made her feel exposed. But this man doing it...

It felt like the beginning of a dangerous game played with loaded dice where the outcome was predetermined, inevitable. Irresistible.

'Thank you,' she said after a moment. 'I was just decompressing. If you want to go up, that's fine.'

'Okay.' He nodded but he didn't move and neither did she. They just kept staring at one another.

'Actually, I wanted to thank you,' he said after another beat of silence.

'For what?'

'I lost the thread earlier with Checco and my uncle. You had my back.'

She shrugged. 'Your back is my back.'

'You kept your head. I'm grateful.'

'How did we do? Did we pass? I couldn't tell.'

'I think so.'

He looked tired, but then it must have been as stressful for him as it was for her. Maybe more so.

'You passed anyway. You were more than a match for

them. Even though they were incredibly provoking, particularly Checco, you didn't let them get under your skin.'

She remembered the edge to Ettore's voice as he'd warned his cousin. The memory of how he had turned and silenced the other man scraped over her skin.

'You did,' she said softly.

His expression didn't alter but she felt something shift between them.

'It's complicated.'

She thought about Oscar and his bouts of despair and drunkenness. 'Families are like that.'

'What shall I do with these?'

He was holding out the pins and she forced herself to take them. As her fingers brushed against the palm of his hand, her pulse surged forward with a whumping sound like a tide curving under a cliff and she was so sure that he could hear it and understand what he was hearing that, instead of picking the pins up, she managed to knock several of them onto the grass.

'Sorry.'

He crouched down, his fingers rifling through the dense blades, and she was almost tempted to help him. But she had watched enough romcoms to know that dropping-things-and-picking-them-up was a classic meet-cute scenario and, after what had happened in London, she didn't want him getting the wrong idea.

Or her?

'You didn't drop them,' she said as calmly as she could with that question repeating inside her head. 'I did.'

'I wasn't apologising for that. I was apologising for yesterday. For how I acted. How I overreacted. I said things I didn't mean.'

He was apologising. She felt oddly fragile.

'And I said things I did. I wasn't pretending. You were bleeding. I was worried.'

'I know.' His gaze moved past her as if he was searching for something in the darkness. Or maybe seeing it.

'I know,' he said again. 'I was worried about you, too. I thought…' He hesitated. 'It reminded me of what happened with Edoardo. He was the heir, before me,' he said simply. 'And then he wasn't.'

Wasn't. Small words, big meaning.

'What happened to him?'

'He was killed on the estate. Riding one of the dirt bikes. He lost control and the bike hit a tree. I was with him when it happened. I can still hear the noise in my head…'

She felt him flinch inside, heard the splintering sound again. And she had been simply messing about. No wonder he'd overreacted.

'Were you on the bike too?' The thought appalled her.

Ettore shook his head. 'We were on different bikes. I came off as well, but I wasn't as badly hurt. We were both taken to hospital but only one of us woke up.'

Her relief was instant and profound and absolute. And then she felt guilty for being so relieved that Ettore was the one to wake up.

'I'm so sorry, Ettore.'

'I am too. You would have liked him. Everyone liked Edo. He was funny and charming and a bit of a rogue.'

'How were you hurt?'

He lifted up his shirt and she saw that his stomach was dappled with patches of paler skin. Scar tissue. 'I was lucky. I got dragged along by the bike so there was a lot of superficial grazing.' He turned, and she saw similar patches on his back. 'I had minor concussion, and I broke my arm, but other than that I was fine. But then I was wearing a helmet.'

She reached out to touch the scar on his stomach and this time he didn't jerk away. 'When did it happen?'

'The September after we split up.'

Just a month after they had split up, to be precise. She felt suddenly queasy. She had hated him then as you hated someone you loved still. Now that love had faded to indifference and yet, of course it hurt to picture him lying injured in a hospital or standing, pale and dark suited with his arm in a sling, at his brother's funeral.

He looked pale now, and there was a tension in his shoulders that looked painful and, without thinking, she stepped forward and slid her arms around his back.

'I'm so sorry, Ettore. For you and your family.'

She felt him hesitate and then his arms tightened around her.

'It was a terrible shock for everyone. My mother had a stroke after the funeral; she died three weeks later and that's when my sister decided to go travelling. I think it was all too much for her. When she left, my dad just stayed in his room.'

So he had been alone with his grief.

'It must have been so awful for you.'

'It was hard. The estate still needed to be managed. We employ sixty people. I couldn't just take a step back.'

'And you didn't. You kept it all going.'

Loosening his arms, he stepped back and stared down at her, his eyes lingering on her mouth before rising to meet hers. She could feel the heat of his skin, see the faint trace of stubble along his jawline.

'Just about. But I think that's probably enough about my family for one day. I know you want to decompress so I'll leave you in peace. Don't stay out too late, I think it's going to rain.'

But he didn't move. Instead he just stood there, his eyes locked on hers, his dark lashes shielding his thoughts. But she could read them anyway. Could feel them pulling her in as his eyes slid back to her mouth.

'You don't have to go…'

Her heart thudded against her ribs as she spoke and she felt his pulse still.

Everything stilled. There was a tension in the air like an intake of breath.

The sun had long since set, but there was enough light from the crescent moon to see his face and she could see the hunger in the taut skin over his cheekbones.

Her breasts tingled.

'You don't have to go,' she said again, and now her voice was scratchy.

There was a beat of silence, then another as she struggled to put together a coherent sentence, one that would express what she was feeling.

What she wanted.

What he wanted?

The question hovered unspoken between them and then as one they answered it. The pins fell from his hands, and he was reaching for her as she stepped towards him.

Their bodies collided, hands gripping and clenching at whatever they could reach, their mouths slotting together just as they had in London. But this was a different kind of kiss. That had been a challenge issued and met. It had been performative and destabilising.

This was a wordless admission of need.

That fine gold thread of hunger between them pulling tight, pulling them closer with powerful, unstoppable magnetic force.

His hand was tight around her waist, the other grasped her head, fingers biting into her scalp. He was kissing her hungrily, hard, hot, open-mouthed kisses that made her grind her hips against his groin.

She moaned. She could feel how hard he was, and she shifted, pushing hard against him, trying to soothe the pulse hammering between her thighs. He made a rough noise in the back of his throat and then he was pushing up her dress, his hands lifting her up and—

'Wait.'

He had jerked his head back and he was staring at her, breathing raggedly, his eyes unfocused.

Not understanding, thinking he wanted to move more into the darkness, she reached for him,

'No, Dulcie, stop.'

And then slowly, inexorably, he stepped backwards, and her body swayed a little as he let her go.

'Ettore?'

He took a deep breath, pressing his hands together as though in prayer.

'Go back inside.'

She stared at him in confusion. There was a coolness in his voice, and she felt it wind over her skin even as her face burned.

'What do you mean? Are you serious?' Her heart banged inside her chest, and she was suddenly conscious of her bare feet and her shaking hands and how the neckline of her dress was lower than her nipples.

'Intensely.'

A drop of rain splashed on her face. Then another and there was a faint, warning rumble from overhead.

'Go back inside, Dulcie,' he repeated and then he turned and walked into the darkness as the rain started to fall, smashing against the leaves with the same force as the hail that had fallen in Paris.

She made it back to her bedroom, and she stood by the window for a long time. But she didn't see Ettore come back, and after an hour, when her dress was dry, she stripped off and got into bed.

Her body was taut and twitchy with frustration, and her head kept replaying the moment when Ettore had pulled away, so it was impossible to fall asleep. Which was why she heard the click of his door about an hour later.

And as she lay in the darkness, her body rigid, her mouth still trembling from his kisses, she didn't think she had ever felt more alone. Or more unhappy.

CHAPTER SEVEN

'THANK YOU SO much for coming today, Signore, Signora. Everyone is very excited for your visit.'

Giulia Rossi, the manager of the residential care home, beamed at Dulcie and Ettore. 'And on behalf of all the staff and residents at St Maria, may I offer our congratulations? *Auguri! Che la gioia abitarvi ogni giorno e l'amore accompagnarvi per tutta la vita.*'

'Thank you.' Ettore smiled, and Dulcie felt his hand press lightly around her waist. 'Signora Rossi is wishing us joy, and love in our life for ever.'

Dulcie smiled. 'Thank you. That's very kind of you.'

And optimistic on so many levels, she thought, watching Ettore shake hands with the assembled staff.

Joy and love were not part of their marriage.

And neither was sex.

A wave of humiliation skittered across her skin as her brain unhelpfully replayed the moment when Ettore had reared away from her as if he were a vampire and she were holding out a bunch of garlic.

It was so embarrassing. All of it. Her physical response to his body, the fact that it had gone so far, and, worst of all, that he had been the one to put a stop to it.

And yet she could understand why it had happened. Could almost forgive herself.

Surely it was the most likely outcome if you put two former lovers in close proximity and said 'pretend to be married'. Sex with an ex was a thing. And seeing him every day had churned everything up. Made it harder to know what was real and what was pretend. And yes, she had allowed the past to overlap the present and blur into something that felt real and current and mutual.

And it was mutual, briefly, she thought as she remembered the urgency of Ettore's hands and mouth.

But even if there was a connection that went beyond this marriage of convenience, clearly it was not one that Ettore wanted to acknowledge. He might have struck the match with her, but he had swiftly extinguished the flame.

Now, though, was not the time to be thinking about any of this. Some people had real problems that were not of their own making.

The day had not got off to the most promising start. In fact, she had spent most of the morning alone. Which would have been a blessing only a few days earlier, but that was before she had made an idiot of herself with Ettore.

He had joined her for breakfast momentarily but as soon as he could, he had made his excuses and left. His excuses had been vague enough that she knew he simply wanted to avoid her. And even though she had spent the last few days trying to avoid him, it didn't feel like an equal trade.

She had still been sitting at the breakfast table some twenty minutes later, trying not to remember the look on his face when she asked him not to leave last night, when he had suddenly reappeared.

‘I have an appointment this morning at St Maria’s. It’s been in the diary for months.’ He pushed a folder across the table. ‘If you’d rather stay here and just relax by the pool, I quite understand But if you’d like to come with me, I’d like that.’

Was he ill? She felt swamped with panic but when she opened the folder, she realised that it wasn’t a hospital, as she’d assumed from the name, but a children’s home.

It was a coincidence. Obviously, but it still made her fingers bite into her thighs beneath the table.

Oscar’s time in care was a permanent reminder of her betrayal. It was because of her. She had failed to protect him. She had abandoned him, knowing that her mother couldn’t cope. But this was a chance to see for herself what Oscar had experienced.

Now, as Signora Rossi led them into what looked like an oversized family home, Dulcie said slowly, ‘I imagine that joy and love are very important to your work here.’

She nodded. ‘They are. We have children who have experienced great suffering in their lives. Children who have lost one or both parents. Children with parents in prison or who are struggling with addiction and poverty.’

Pushing back against the unwieldy mass of guilt and regret and recrimination and shame that she carried with her at all times, Dulcie nodded.

Was this the kind of place where Oscar might have stayed? She had no real idea, she realised with a distant jolt. Her brother didn’t so much refuse to talk about his time in care as shrug it off. But she knew that at least half his childhood had been spent in children's homes with the occasional, unsuccessful stay with foster parents.

'Is this a typical *casa-famiglia*, Signora Rossi?' she asked as they walked into a large, bright kitchen. Turning, she screwed up her face apologetically. 'Sorry, am I saying that right?'

'Perfectly. And please, call me Giulia. How long have you been learning Italian?'

'I started about two years ago, but then I stopped and now I'm trying again, but I do find some of the combinations of letters difficult to pronounce and my vocabulary is currently limited to ordering food and complaining about it before I ask for the bill.'

She felt Ettore's gaze seek her out and she fixed her eyeline on the large pine table in the centre of the room.

Signora Rossi laughed. 'I remember it well. When I was learning English, I thought I would be forever ordering fish and chips and a pot of tea.'

'Your English is perfect.'

'My husband is English, and we lived in Oxford for ten years so it should be perfect, but I still speak with an accent.' She lowered her voice. 'One of the best ways to learn a language is to watch TV. Just watch your favourite shows with Italian subtitles or Italian shows with English subtitles. Talking to children is also a good way to learn.'

'It is? Why's that?'

'Children are less self-conscious.'

Dulcie blinked. It was Ettore who had answered, not Giulia. Looking up, she found his gaze resting intently on her face.

'They're more forgiving of grammatical errors and imperfect pronunciation. They won't try to correct you, they'll just talk, which helps you learn the rhythm and flow of a language.'

'Exactly that.' Giulia nodded. 'Your husband knows what he is talking about. Now, to answer your question, St Maria is quite typical, although we are lucky to have extra financial support from the Marchesi family, so we've been able to create a games room and an outdoor play area.'

'This is lovely,' Dulcie said as they reached the living room. 'It feels just like a family home.' Or what a family home should feel like. There were sofas and shelves with books and a TV.

Giulia nodded. 'Traditionally, in the past, these kinds of homes used to be more institutionalised. But as a country, we moved away from larger residential buildings to something smaller scale with a more family-oriented atmosphere. Which reminds me, we were hoping that you might stay and have lunch with us.'

The children, supervised by some of the staff, made pasta from scratch and a tomato sauce.

'*Ricchie e macurroni*. It's a local dish. Every family in every village has their own version and they are kept secret and handed down from generation to generation. And they all swear theirs is the best. But I think this is the best one.'

Dulcie took a mouthful. It tasted familiar. 'It's delicious.'

After lunch, Dulcie did some colouring with the younger children and Ettore went off to play football before being dragged into the gaming room.

Signora Rossi smiled. 'He is very good with the children, especially the older boys. They look forward to his visits.'

'So, he comes here often?'

She had sensed that the staff and children recognised Ettore but as the older woman nodded, she realised that what she had taken for politeness was in fact genuine affection.

'The Marchesi family has been generous.'

The older woman paused as if she was assembling her words with care. 'It was your husband's idea to set up a mentorship scheme with local businesses, including Castiglione Fiana. They offer work experience and apprenticeships to children from St Maria when they leave the home. But that's not why the children like him.'

Dulcie felt her gaze pull towards the teenage boy who had watched the tour from the sidelines, tugging at the zip of his hoodie. When they had arrived, he had been at the edges of the room, his shoulders hunched, hands clenched in his trouser pockets. His body language was completely different now. He seemed looser, more relaxed, largely, she suspected, because of the man sitting next to him, a game console in his hand, his muscular body dwarfing the beanbag he was sitting on.

She felt an inappropriate kick of heat that almost knocked her off her feet. There weren't many men who could pull off that look. But Ettore looked as if he were posing for the cover photo of a men's magazine.

After yesterday's fiasco in the garden, she'd honestly thought that weird undercurrent of heat, of attraction, would be extinguished. But it was still here, simmering away beneath the surface. For her, anyway.

'Why do they like him?' she asked. She couldn't help herself, but she had an excuse because she was in character.

Giulia smiled.

'They like that he keeps his promises. He turns up when he says he will and that's important for these children. He listens to them and, most importantly, he treats them like he would treat anyone. They don't get that very often. And he doesn't try to be cool. But apparently, he's "cracked".'

Dulcie frowned. 'Is that good?'

Giulia's mouth twitched. 'I believe so.'

Dulcie was sorry to leave St Maria's. The children came out to wave them off and she kept thinking about Oscar and his experience of being taken into care. He was five years old the first time it happened. Who had dropped him off? Had he cried? What had it felt like being looked after by strangers? To be left behind? To be alone with his fear and his pain?

He was alone now, she thought, her pulse hammering in her ears. And like her mother, she had failed to look after him, to fix him. She had failed him in so many ways and yet other people spent their lives looking after children with care and dedication and love. Real, undeniable love, she thought, remembering how the children had clung to Giulia as they left.

She felt suddenly split open with grief and guilt and self-loathing.

'What are you thinking about?' Ettore's voice cut across her thoughts, and she glanced up at him, her body tensing, terrified that the words might spill from her mouth.

'I was trying to remember what you put in that sauce,' she lied. 'It was your recipe, wasn't it?'

He stared at her for a moment. 'You remembered,' he said finally.

She nodded. 'You cooked it for me the first time you came to my flat in London. You made the pasta as well. I was very impressed.'

'I can't take credit for the recipe. It actually belongs to Valentina's grandmother.'

'I thought those recipes were handed down through the generations like family heirlooms.'

'They are, but I took Valentina over to Lecce to visit her grandmother and we got talking.'

She thought back to the silver-framed photo she had seen of Ettore, solemn-eyed and unsmiling, tall for his age, standing between the brother who looked nothing like him and the sister who so resembled him.

They were a good-looking family with their dark eyes and patrician profiles. But, now she had met his extended family, there was something that set Ettore apart. Those gold eyes maybe or the intensity of his focus when he looked at you as if there were nothing in the universe that mattered except you.

No wonder Valentina's grandmother had cast aside centuries of silence and shared the secrets of her cookbook with him.

'And she took a shine to you. I'm guessing that must happen all the time to the Marchesi heir apparent.'

He waited a moment, and she knew that he was forming sentences in his head, editing them, maybe deleting them, but then he nodded.

'My name has brought benefits, but since the *Costituzione della Repubblica Italiana*—the creation of the constitution in Italy—there has been no state recognition of my title. However, many noble families like mine continue to use their titles socially, as a matter of tradition and custom.'

She thought of Checco. Over dinner he had been charming, easy company. But there was an arrogant tilt to his chin when he spoke not just to the staff but to his girlfriend.

'But you don't.'

The change in him was subtle. There was no flaring of nostrils, just that slight tightening of his mouth and she knew why. It was because he had only recently become the heir apparent and under circumstances that he would rather forget.

And it hit her then that she'd found out more about Ettore in the last few days than she had during the entire time they were together two years ago.

'That's probably another reason why the kids all think you're cool.'

His forehead creased. 'I'm pretty sure the kids think I'm a fossil.'

'*Al contrario*, Signor Marchesi,' she said with a flourish, enjoying the gleam in his eye as she practised her Italian. 'Giulia told me that they think you're "cracked", which is allegedly high praise from a group of teenage boys.'

He laughed then, and it was so genuine and unforced, so unlike the artificiality of the previous few days that she laughed too, and something that had been hard and frozen inside her chest softened and thawed a little. She felt loose and warm as his dark golden gaze hovered on her face.

'It's gamer slang for good.' His eyes met hers. 'Although they might have downgraded me on my performance today. I was a little off my game. Then again, maybe they gave me a pass because my wife is so beautiful.'

The skin of her face felt scorched.

'Did they say that?'

'No. But I was thinking it.'

His mouth crooked into a smile that made it a little hard to breathe and then he reached over and smoothed a stray strand of her hair behind her ear and every single cell in her body shivered into a state of high alert.

'Your Italian accent is excellent, by the way. You're rolling your r's beautifully.'

'Grazie,' she said, inclining her head in a perfect imitation of his uncle, and was instantly rewarded as his smile reached his eyes.

She felt a breeze and she stared round dazedly, shocked to realise that not only had they stopped moving but Silvio had managed to get out of the car and walk around it to open her door all without her even noticing.

Judging by the expression on Ettore's face, he hadn't noticed either. Heart juddering like the floor polisher she used to clean the parquet at the college in Cambridge, she watched him draw back his hand, flattening it against the palm of his other hand.

As if he needed that pressure to stop himself from reaching out again.

Just as he had done yesterday evening in the moonlight.

And it felt like fire under her skin, and the heat of it lingered like sunburn as she stepped out of the car and waited for Ettore to join her. She felt his hand against the small of her back as they walked inside.

'I'm just going to check on my father.'

'Okay.' She nodded. 'I might go and take a quick shower.'

His pupils dilated and she had to resist the urge to squirm beneath his gaze as she had a sudden, sharp-edged memory of his body beside hers, water trickling down his neck and shoulders as his hands moved to cup her breasts…

'I'll join you in a moment.'

Their eyes locked together, and she swallowed audibly.

'I meant, I'll join you upstairs,' he said in a rough whisper that vibrated through her as if her body were a tubular bell, and he took a small, involuntary step towards her, then stopped.

For a few pulsing half-seconds, neither of them moved.

They stood like statues, frozen, separately bewitched by how that skin-prickling gravitational energy between them was suddenly bright and hard and undeniable. And then Valentina appeared, and the spell snapped, and Dulcie remembered how to breathe and smile and move her legs again.

She made her way upstairs, her head spinning madly.

It was hard to believe that it was still the same day as the one that had started this morning. Waking, she had felt taut and thwarted and trapped, and, rolling out of bed, she had been on the verge of storming into the dressing room and hurling all her clothes into the suitcase and then shinning back down the wisteria outside her window. Only the thought that she was helping Oscar had stopped her from doing so.

Oscar.

She had checked her phone obsessively every day since

her brother had gone into the rehab centre even though she knew that he wasn't allowed his phone. Today was the first day she had forgotten to do so and, feeling horribly guilty, she pulled it out and saw instantly that there was a voice message from Oscar. The floor yawed sideways as if she were standing on the deck of a ship in a rough sea and she clicked on the message and listened.

'Dulcie, I can't do this.' Her brother's voice was high and ragged with panic and fear, and she felt her stomach somersault. Her mouth tasted sour. She thought she was going to throw up.

'I can't do it. It's too hard. You have to get me out of here, please, Dulcie, please—'

The message got cut off and her fingers moved clumsily over the screen as if she might be able to reach Oscar and pull him to safety.

'What's wrong? Has something happened?'

For a moment, she didn't understand that Ettore was even in the room, let alone talking to her. Everything around her was reduced to its most basic form. The red of the curtains, the rectangular outline of the rug beneath her feet.

'It's Oscar, he called me— He sounded desperate.'

'His body is readjusting to sobriety. He will be desperate.'

Ettore's face stilled, hardened a fraction like the first crystals of ice hardening the surface of a lake in winter and there was a dark edge of impatience to his voice that she hadn't heard all day as he took a step towards her. 'I thought he wasn't supposed to have contact with anyone until the withdrawal stage was over.'

'He's not but he must have got hold of his phone somehow, he's upset…' Her heart was suddenly a hot, slippery shape, flopping against her ribs, but the rigidity in Ettore's face was spreading to his body. He was becoming a fortress in front of her eyes.

'So, you spoke to him?'

His voice cut her panicky thoughts in two, and she glanced up at him, bitterness swelling inside her because this was his fault. He had made her choose again, and she had chosen wrongly.

'No. He left a message. Not that you care.'

His expression didn't change but his eyes stilled on her face.

'Of course I care. Not least, because you're obviously upset.' She watched as he turned and closed the door softly, and she felt a rush of fury, because even now, when her brother was in despair, he was worried about someone hearing them argue and wrecking his precious pantomime.

'All you care about is yourself. You don't care about me, and you don't care about Oscar. You couldn't wait to get him shut up in that clinic and now he's—' Her voice broke, and she pressed her hand against her mouth.

'Dulcie.'

He was beside her now and she stumbled backwards.

'I need my suitcase.'

She turned and walked swiftly into the dressing room, yanking her bag from where it had been neatly stowed. Pulse thundering, she pulled clothes randomly from the shelves.

'What are you doing?' Ettore was blocking her exit.

'I'm leaving. Unlock the safe. I need my passport. Give me my passport.'

'You can't just leave.'

'Why not? You did. You just walked out on me.'

'I'm not walking out now.' His hands were suddenly holding her shoulders and maybe it was that or maybe it was his words, but she felt the bag slip from her fingers.

'I'm not going anywhere, but I can't help if I don't know what's going on.'

'You can't help.' She shook off his hands and took an unsteady step backwards. 'You don't know what it's like living with an addict. You don't understand how relentless they are. How determined they are to hurt themselves. How every morning, you wake up wondering how you're going to get through the day, how you're going to get *them* through the day without everything imploding.'

'And it's every day,' Ettore said quietly. 'Every day you have to stay alert and focused. You can never relax, except sometimes you have to. Sometimes you want to, only then you have to deal with the consequences. Because they're your responsibility.'

Ettore breathed out unsteadily. Dulcie was staring at him in shock and something like panic. But then it wasn't often that somebody read your mind. Of course, it was more than simple mind-reading. He knew exactly what she was feeling because he had walked in her shoes.

She cleared her throat. 'How do you know that?'

'Many great dynasties have been rumoured to have a curse. In Italy, it is my family who have been troubled by tragedy. But the big stuff, the visible stuff, that's all in the public domain. Nothing to see there. Unfortunately, my family also specialises in behind the scenes chaos. My job is to hide that chaos. To bury the scandals. To clear up their messes. Their titles may be royal. Their behaviour, unfortunately, is less so. And it's been that way since before I can remember.'

Was he really going to do this now? Apparently, yes.

The thought made his hand reach automatically for the back of his neck as it always did when he was stressed. And yet, he didn't feel stressed. Oddly, *al contrario*, in fact, it felt like the right time. Or maybe Dulcie was the right person, the only person who could understand.

'What kind of chaos?' she said now.

'My brother, Edo, was a gambler. I don't mean he liked a flutter on the horses. I mean high-stakes poker games with six-figure buy-ins. There was one year where I pretty much spent every week flying round the world paying off his debts. My uncle keeps a string of mistresses. My father did, too. And then there's my cousins. Checco and his brothers like to get coked up and hang out with the offspring of dodgy businessmen. And by businessmen, I mean gangsters.'

It felt strange after so long spent smoothing over the cracks to suddenly press against them, strange and yet satisfying somehow to watch the veneer splinter and buckle.

'All of them have spent time in very expensive, very discreet clinics in Switzerland. Not like the Dymphna. There's no glossy webpage with testimonials. No group therapy, no communal area. Patients stay in their own villa or apartment and have their own driver, housekeeper, chef and live-in therapist, as well as daily one-on-one sessions with a team of psychiatrists, doctors, nurses, yoga teachers, masseuses, nutritionists, hypnotherapists and trauma therapists.'

'But it all looks so perfect.' Dulcie seemed stunned.

'When I saw the castle, I thought that's why you didn't want Oscar around. But that wasn't the reason, was it?'

It wasn't. But better to let Dulcie believe it was the reason she was reaching for, than share the truth. Shaking his head, he reached forward and stroked her cheek. 'Sometimes, it's overwhelming. I love my family, but they are alcoholics, sex addicts, drug addicts, gamblers. So, I think I can help you. I'd like to help.'

He turned and unlocked the safe and pulled out Dulcie's passport.

'And if you want to leave and go to see Oscar, I won't stop you.'

He thought back to that day when Oscar had turned up, his eyes glazed, his speech slurred. Dulcie had been beside herself, not outwardly, but her body had been taut like a bowstring, and she'd had eyes only for Oscar. It had been as though she were wearing blinkers, and it was all so horribly familiar to him, that feeling of being invisible and irrelevant, that he had frozen. Frozen Dulcie out.

And he hated that he'd done that. But hating himself wasn't enough. He needed to put things right. To be the husband she had needed then and still needed now.

He held out the passport. 'But if you leave, I'm coming with you.'

'You'd do that for me?'

'You're my wife. And you were my wife two years ago when I let you down.'

She was biting her lip, and the tears she'd been holding back had started streaking her cheeks.

'I don't want to let Oscar down. Not again.'

'I doubt you've ever let him down.' He reached out and stroked her face, but she jerked away.

'But I did. I let him down so badly.'

Her pain pierced him deep inside. 'Maybe it's only bad in your head.'

Her eyes met his briefly and then she shook her head slowly. 'I left him.'

'When?'

'When my parents divorced. My dad asked me to choose between him and my mum.' She pressed her wrist against her mouth. 'I chose my dad because I knew if he left me, I'd never see him again.'

He heard her swallow. 'But that wasn't the only reason. My mum was an alcoholic and when my dad was away on business she'd forget to feed me and Oscar. And I didn't want my friends to meet her because she would drop things and do stupid dances, and I was embarrassed.'

Her hands were shaking. 'I was embarrassed so I chose my dad, and Oscar stayed with my mum. He was only two.'

'How old were you?'

'Seven. But I knew what I was doing was wrong.' She looked up at him angrily as if defying him to contradict her. 'I knew that she couldn't look after him, but I left anyway. And then he ended up in care. Ended up like he is now.'

'You couldn't have known that would happen.'

'But I did. I knew she couldn't cope on her own. I knew because I was the one who bathed him and fed him and put him to bed.'

'What about your dad?'

'He didn't want another baby. He never hurt Oscar or anything like that, but he never picked him up or played with him.'

'How did he end up in care?'

'He didn't go to school for months. She was living in a van by then, moving around all the time. He was so thin when they finally caught up with her and all his clothes were dirty. And I was having ballet lessons and riding lessons and going to boarding school.'

Ettore could hear a roaring noise in his ears.

Years of going to the *casa-famiglia* had taught him that some people were not meant to have children, but it still shocked and appalled him. Angered him too. But his feelings weren't important here.

'You didn't do anything wrong. You were a child. Your father should never have asked you to choose.'

But you did. The accusation reverberated inside his head, blunt and undeniably true. But he would deal with the guilt and remorse it provoked later.

'And I should have refused. But I knew my dad would just leave us behind. Leave me behind. I was thinking about myself.'

'Because you weren't an adult. Okay, your mum wasn't able to do the right thing, but Oscar had two parents. It didn't matter if your dad didn't want him. He was his responsibility.'

Reaching out, Ettore touched her cheek gently and this time she didn't jerk away.

'Did you not see Oscar after that?'

'I asked if we could see them but my dad said that my mum's situation had changed and that she couldn't have me in her life any more. I thought she'd remarried. But she'd actually gone into a clinic and Oscar was in care. My dad knew that but he made me think that she had a new husband so that I wouldn't ask him to look after his own son. He refused to do it. I was twenty-one when I found that out. We argued and I said I was going to find my brother and he cut me off.'

'And you did find him. And you've been taking care of him ever since,' Ettore said gently.

She stiffened and then he felt her body soften against his. 'It's okay. He's getting help. We're not going to give up on him. Whatever it takes, however long it takes, you'll be there and I'll be there too.'

He pulled her closer, held her close for a long time, until finally she shifted against his chest and looked up at him. 'What do you think we should do?'

'Honestly? I think he needs help and he's getting it. But detoxing is hard. You have to face the world without your drug of choice. And that's scary. But he's done the hardest part, Dulcie. Taking responsibility is the hardest part. And Oscar can't change unless he keeps accepting that responsibility for himself. If he sees you, he'll have the hardest part to do again.' He hesitated. 'But we don't have to decide here and now. The first thing we need to do is talk to the clinic director.'

It took several hours to resolve. They spoke to Elaine O'Neill and then to several of Oscar's therapists. Ettore joined in the call and Dulcie found his input supportive and constructive. He asked questions and listened to the answers and then asked pertinent follow-up questions. He also asked for the conversation to be written up so that Dulcie could review it.

The consensus was that Oscar's reaction was normal. Distressing but normal.

The conclusion was that he would remain in the

clinic, and they would send Dulcie regular updates on his progress.

'Are you happy with that?' Ettore asked her.

She nodded. 'Yes. Are you?'

'I think the clinic is excellent. They clearly know Oscar. And they care about him. If he were my brother I would continue with the treatment but if at any time you change your mind or you want to go to England and talk to Dr O'Neill in person, we'll go back.'

She nodded. 'Thank you. For today. For everything.'

He found her hand, kissed it gently. 'You don't need to thank me. I'm just pleased I could help. Because I didn't help before, did I?'

'You didn't know about Oscar.'

'I didn't ask about Oscar. I didn't do the right thing. And I'm so sorry for how I acted. I made a bad choice, so many bad choices that day. You made the only sensible one.'

'It didn't feel like it. It felt like I'd been torn in two.'

'It killed me, leaving you. But I was stupid and stubborn.'

'And now?'

'Still stupid and stubborn but more open, more honest.'

'So what are you thinking right now?'

His eyes fixed on her face, clear and gold like sunlight.

'That I wanted you last night,' he said huskily. 'And when we kissed it felt so good, only then I panicked because I wanted so badly for it to be real. And I couldn't handle the idea that it might not be for you.'

His raw admission made her head swim. 'What if it was, if it *is* real for me?'

His breath hitched audibly. 'Then I would be very happy.'

'Happy?'

She reached out and touched his stomach.

'Just happy?'

His fingers moved to touch her face, the thumb pressing against her lips. 'Thrilled. Delighted. Elated. Jubilant. Ecstatic—'

She leaned in and kissed him, and his hand moved to her neck, and he pulled her forward, his tongue pushing between her lips, taking his time.

'Can we take our clothes off now?' she whispered, and he laughed softly against her mouth and his hands joined hers, pulling at zips, fumbling with buttons and belts, both of them clumsy and inexpert with need.

And then they were naked.

She touched his scars and then dropped to her knees and traced their outline with her tongue.

'You're so beautiful,' he murmured, and he was pulling her to her feet, his knuckles sliding in between her thighs, grunting as he felt how wet she was.

He knew exactly where and how to touch her, soothing, teasing her, and she felt a heat sliding up over her belly, knotting and tangling inside her so that she squirmed against his hand, whimpering at the ache that was swelling and building inexorably.

'Can you come inside me? Or is that too fast?'

But he was already pulling her towards the bed. 'Here.' He spun her away from him, and then he lifted her hands and pressed them around the post at the end of the bed. 'Hold onto this.'

She felt her skin tighten as he kissed her throat, and his

hands cupped her breasts, and she lost herself in his touch until suddenly she couldn't stand it any more.

'Ettore, please.'

His hand moved to push her forward, so that her arms were above her head, and she felt him angle up her hips and bottom and he was pushing in slowly, so slowly that she wanted to cry out with frustration.

And then he started to move, and at first the rhythm was wrong and then suddenly they were in time with each other, and he was holding her neck with one hand, sliding the other over her pubic bone to her clitoris.

Her fingers tightened around the post, and she could feel his movements getting larger and more out of control and her own pleasure was building. And then the swollen feeling inside her burst and she cried out as his mouth found hers and he anchored an arm around her waist and thrust inside her one last time.

CHAPTER EIGHT

DULCIE OPENED HER EYES, moving from one kind of darkness to another, seeking the cause of her abrupt awakening. And then she realised what it was.

Ettore was gone.

She didn't try to deny or stifle the disappointment that swelled up inside her chest to fill her ribcage. She was done burying her emotions. And last night, they had risen up inside her like a natural spring.

And out of everything that had happened last night, that was the most surprising part. That despite having clutched her guilt and shame close to her for so many years, telling Ettore the truth about her childhood had been easy.

Not painless, but he had made it easy somehow.

His honesty and support had overwhelmed her, and it had felt like the most natural thing in the world to lean into his hard chest, and for him to stroke her hair and hold her close.

And when he had tilted her face up to his so that his mouth was so temptingly close to hers, how could she not have kissed him?

Or touched his face, his arms, his chest…

She pressed her thighs together around the ache there,

a slide of heat cutting through her like a hot knife through butter as she remembered his fingers pressing hers around the post and the feel of his cock as he thrust inside her.

Afterwards, when he'd held her close, it had felt more than just post-coital satisfaction. It had felt like an admission of something. Of possibilities and the potential for a rearranged world order where this lie they were living wasn't pretence any more.

Because she knew who he was now, and why he had reacted as he had when Oscar had turned up, unannounced, drunk. She had seen his confusion and shock and interpreted it as disapproval. But now she knew that he had seen Oscar as yet another responsibility to add to all his other responsibilities.

She glanced up as the door to the bedroom opened, blinking into the light angling across the floor, and her heart slipped free of its moorings.

It was Ettore.

'You're awake.'

She nodded. 'I just woke up.'

'Good.' He nodded, and the hope rushing through her veins slowed to a trickle. He didn't sound unfriendly, but he didn't sound like the man who had stretched her hands above her head and licked her throat and sucked her nipples into his mouth until she'd begged him to take her.

'I have a couple of calls to make but I'll tell Valentina to bring you up some breakfast.'

'I can—' she began, but he had already closed the door.

She had barely managed to press the remote to open the thick curtains that covered the windows before she heard Valentina knock on the door.

'Buongiorno, Signora.'

'Grazie, Valentina,' she said as the housekeeper placed one of those folding wooden trays that you saw in period dramas across her lap. 'Goodness, what's all this?'

'Scrambled eggs and pancetta. And then some fruit and coffee. Signor Ettore said you'd had a restless night, and you might need something for energy. But I can make something else if you prefer?'

'No, no, no. This is perfect. Truly.'

'*Buon appetito!* Would you like me to bring another cup?'

Dulcie looked up from her tray in confusion, wondering why Valentina was asking her that, and was shocked to see that Ettore had returned. She stared at him mutely, caught in the honeytrap of his golden gaze and that devastatingly beautiful face. As Valentina retreated, she half expected Ettore to follow her. But instead, he murmured something to the housekeeper and then closed the door softly. Dulcie stared at him in silence, waiting for him to disappear through the connecting door back into his room. But he didn't do that either.

Instead, he walked over to the bed.

'Have you eaten?'

He nodded. 'Earlier. I didn't want to wakc you. I thought you needed some sleep.'

'You mean after my restless night?' she said softly. 'Restless?'

She watched his mouth pull up at the corners minutely in a way that made her skin feel hot and shivery and her fingers reached for the edge of the sheet, tightening it around her body.

'I thought it covered a multitude of—'

'Sins?'

His eyes found hers and he looked at her with hypnotised intensity for what was arguably an unnecessarily long time, and yet every second that passed felt essential. 'I was going to say interpretations. Although I think I prefer sins.'

Heat blossomed between her thighs.

He was replaying their night together. She knew because she was replaying it too and, meeting his melting, gold gaze, she was dizzy, light-headed.

'I just wanted—' he began.

'You don't have to—' she said.

They both stopped at once. 'We need to talk,' he said after a moment. 'But eat first.'

She had lost her appetite, but then she remembered what that police officer had said to her when Oscar was arrested for causing a disturbance. She had sat at the police station all night waiting for him to be released and one of the officers had taken pity on her and brought her a bacon roll and a cup of tea. 'If it's going to be a long day, I have a fry-up and a cup of tea to fortify myself,' he'd said. 'I can't offer you a fry-up, but I can manage a butty and a brew.'

Breathing out unsteadily, she nodded. 'Okay, but could you just sit down?'

He sat on the bed beside her, and she ate her bacon and eggs, nibbled at some fruit and then drank her coffee. As she put down her cup, she forced herself to meet his gaze.

'So, about last night…'

'I don't want to talk about that,' he said firmly. 'I want to talk about today.'

She could feel her body tensing. 'What's there to talk about? We had sex. It's what married people do. Unmarried ones, too, as it happens.'

'I don't want to talk about sex either.'

Because it was a one-off. He had wanted closure and—

'I want to talk about us. This. This arrangement we made.'

It was like being blindfolded with her head on a block, waiting for the axe to fall. Except she wasn't blindfolded. She could see his face and was going to have to look into his eyes as he swung the axe.

'Are you saying you want to end it?'

'No.' His gaze burned into her, his voice fierce and so adamant that she almost flinched. And there were no words to describe what that one word spoken with such assurance did to her then. How it carved through her, hollowing her out with need and hope and fear and yearning all at once.

'That's not what I want at all.'

He reached out and pulled her towards him, gently at first and then more roughly, drawing her closer until his lips found hers and he was kissing her then, an open-mouthed, unbound, demanding kiss, his hand tightening in her hair, his mouth hungry, clumsy with hunger as if they hadn't just spent the night with his body in hers and on hers in a feverish waking dream of touch and relief and release.

She whimpered against his mouth, arching into his body, her nipples hardening as they grazed his chest.

'What I want is to spend some time alone with you. What I want is it to be just the two of us. Because I am your husband and you are my wife. But my family are here and they're not exactly shy and sensitive. So, I think we need to go some other place. I think what we need is a honeymoon.'

* * *

Ettore felt Dulcie's body stiffen with shock.

Which was fair.

He had brought her here to Italy to perform a charade of 'happy ever after' for his family but a honeymoon had not been mentioned for the very obvious reason that it was extraneous to requirements.

It didn't feel extraneous now.

It felt like an imperative.

He could see a pulse beating frantically against the delicate skin of her throat and he stared at it, mesmerised, trying to decipher her answer as if her pulse were beating out a message in Morse code.

'And this is so that everyone thinks that we're together.' He could see the wound in her eyes; a wound he had given her. 'You want to give them concrete proof that our marriage is real.'

'I don't care what everyone else thinks. And it's not about proving our marriage is real. This is about us. It's about this thing, this thing between us that we don't have to prove is real. Because we both feel it, *dolcezza*.'

Dolcezza. Sweetness.

That was what he used to call her, a play on her name and because she made him think of spun sugar. She drew the eye in the same way. There was a lightness about her that made people curious and intrigued.

It had started in Paris that first morning they finally left his room, five days after she had knocked on his door, a need she had never felt for any other man blazing inside her as the storm roared through the empty streets. They might have walked into the hotel as two strangers but now they were a couple. Walking the streets, with the pale, serene sun tracking their progress, it felt like the dawn of a new world. Dulcie and Ettore's world.

There was no evidence of the hailstones that had stopped their flights, but there were signs of the damage they had caused. Boarded-up windows. Torn awnings. Broken slates on the pavement. Cars with dented bonnets.

Only then they walked past a patisserie and there was a Paris-Brest behind the cracked window, topped with cream and a shimmering halo of spun sugar, as delicate and ethereal as stardust and yet it had survived the storm.

Dulcie wanted to stop and look at it, and he understood why. Because he was as fascinated by her as she was by those gossamer-fine strands of sugar. So fascinated that he found it hard to look away.

Pushing aside his memories, he fixed his eyes on her face, the warm, damp, feminine scent of her enveloping him.

It was still hard now.

Her blue eyes searched his face. 'Will it work?'

'What? You and me and a room to ourselves with no interruptions?'

She smiled. 'What about room service?'

He touched her cheek. 'I know it feels like a big deal, but we've done all the hard stuff. How many couples have gone through what we have? We know everything about each other.'

'What about all of this?'

'The castle? It survived the Roman Empire, pirates, the Ottomans, Mussolini and Second World War bombers. I think it can keep standing for a few days without me.'

'I meant running the estate, and all your noblesse oblige stuff.'

'Gianni is perfectly competent, and my family can pick up the slack. As for my obligations, I intend to focus all my attention and resources on you.'

Her pupils flared, and he felt his own body snap to attention.

'And if we need to get back for Oscar, I will take you.'

She wasn't sure. He could see the conflict in her eyes, the battle between self and other, safety and risk, sense and desire. He had fought the same battle, and desire had championed. As he heard her soft 'okay' he lowered his mouth to hers with a soft groan of relief.

'It'll be okay. He's in good hands.'

'He's been through so much.' Her voice stumbled. 'And he doesn't have anyone looking out for him, except me.'

'He has us.'

He saw the sheen of tears in her eyes, and he felt a fierce rage with a world that blithely encouraged the goal of marriage and parenthood without adequately equipping people with the skills to make those life-changing decisions work. Dulcie was such a good person, but she had been forced into making a choice that she should never have had to make as a child. And the consequences for Oscar were far-reaching and devastating.

And then he had forced her to make a near identical choice.

His stomach twisted. He could still remember how Dulcie had braced herself that day in London when he'd asked her to choose between him and her brother.

Except, he didn't need to remember it. Growing up, that feeling of tightness in his jaw, neck, shoulders, back, as if his body was tensing up to absorb a blow, had been so much a part of him then that he'd thought it was normal.

By the time he realised it wasn't, he had developed coping strategies like the ones Oscar's psychiatrist had mentioned. Ways to block out or numb the pain and the shame of being superfluous, second-best, and, worst of all, saved.

'Why did I have to lose him? Why couldn't it have been you?'

His mother's voice, cracking with pain and despair, reverberated inside his head, and he flinched at the sound.

'What is it?'

He stared down at Dulcie, his pulse lurching. There was an indent in her forehead, just above her nose, and her eyes were a soft blue that washed over him like a gentle wave. She was worried about him. And the fact that she cared made him lose his bearings momentarily.

Made him momentarily consider telling her the truth. That his father merely tolerated him. Much as he would tolerate an efficient maître d' who would get him the best table in a restaurant. That his mother had not just blamed him for his brother's death, she would have preferred him to die instead.

'Ettore?'

'It's nothing. I was just wondering whether or not to tell you where we're going?'

'You've chosen where we're going?'

'I have. But it's a surprise.'

'I like surprises.' She shifted her weight, sliding her leg across his lap to straddle him, and he stared at her naked body, his brain a perfect blank slate, his cock hardening with such speed and intensity that he was glad he was sitting down.

'I hope it's not too long a flight.' She leaned into him,

her mouth brushing against his, and his hands moved automatically to cup her breasts, and he felt her breath snatch in her throat as his thumbs made contact with her nipples. They were already swollen and quivering slightly and now it was his breath that snatched audibly.

'Any particular reason?' Heat slid over his skin as her mouth curved up into a sweet, head-spinning smile.

'Just that I get restless on long flights.' He felt her hand close around the pulsing head of his cock and her unfaltering touch made him twitch with impatience, his muscles, his breath, his blood swelling and reaching towards her.

'Really, relentlessly restless.'

The *s*'s curled over his skin.

'That's okay. We're taking the jet,' he said hoarsely, his hands sliding down over her body to cradle her bottom. 'There's a bedroom on board. You can be as restless as you need.'

Dulcie was in the window seat, but as he heard the clunk of the landing gear, Ettore leaned forward, his gaze tracking over the large urban sprawl as the jet made its descent. They had been in the air for only two hours. But despite the shortness of the flight, they had both been restless and almost as soon as the steward had told them that they could unfasten their seat belts, they had retreated to the bedroom.

'How are you feeling?' He leaned in to press a kiss on her throat and she closed the guidebook he'd given her on the flight, and turned towards him, her lips parting into that smile, the sweet, curling smile that felt like sunlight on his skin.

'Tired. Happy.' She kissed him softly on the mouth. They were kissing a lot. Touching a lot since yesterday.

'Excited. Happy.' She kissed him on the mouth again. 'Hungry. Happy.' Her gaze shifted to the window then back to his face. 'I can't believe we're going to Paris.'

There was no shortage of honeymoon destinations around the globe. And he had briefly considered some of them, but his mind had kept circling back to Paris. Not just because it was a beautiful, romantic city. It was their city. The place where they met. The place where they were just Ettore and Dulcie. On their first visit two years ago, all they had wanted and needed was each other and a king-size bed.

Maybe that was all they needed now to make this work.

Liar.

Coward.

What they needed—what Dulcie needed—was for him to tell her the truth. As she had told him her truth. Silently, he formed sentences inside his head, testing them out, comparing them as if he were actually going to say them out loud.

Liar.

Coward.

How could he tell her the truth? She had loved him once, then hated him, and then hated him some more when he'd turned up in her life and twisted their marriage into something to fit his agenda. But she had never pitied him. And he couldn't stomach that. He could picture her face, how she would avoid his eyes when hers was always the most challenging gaze.

Nothing could change the past, not even the truth. But he could make amends. And that was what this trip to

Paris was about. Not unburdening himself to a woman who had shouldered enough burdens in her life.

Let her have Paris. Let her have some unalloyed days without having to worry about yet another dysfunctional man.

'So, you're pleased.' He knew she was, but he just wanted to hear her say it.

'You know I am. I would have been happy going anywhere with you, but Paris is just perfect.'

It was perfect, Dulcie thought, three hours later as they finally left the hotel.

They hadn't had a honeymoon two years ago. Somehow, organically, they had decided it would be best to wait and then, of course, they had argued and everything had imploded.

At the time, even more so now, she'd assumed Ettore had wanted to wait because he was trying to process his actions. And she had agreed to wait because she hadn't told Oscar she was getting married.

She hadn't wanted to lie to her brother, but their relationship was still so new then. They had only just reconnected, and Oscar still found it so hard to trust that every day he tested her. She'd tried to reassure him, but getting married would make him question her commitment, which was why she hadn't invited him to the wedding. She'd felt wretched about it. But it was too great a risk because she hadn't been entirely sure of how he'd react. Or maybe she'd known exactly how he'd react.

How would he react to this version of her marriage? Her eyes dropped to the ring on her finger and then to the sapphire and diamond bracelet on her wrist.

Before she went to Puglia, she had assumed Oscar would never find out. That the marriage would be over. But if the marriage was over that would mean that Edoardo had died.

The thought made her feel sick with self-loathing.

But if the marriage wasn't over then she would have to tell Oscar, and that made her feel sick with panic.

'Where would you like to go first?'

Ettore's hand wrapped around hers, and she looked up, her heart pounding at the sight of him.

'Actually, could you choose? My brain is still playing catch-up.'

'You need some food. Let's grab some lunch and we can take it from there.'

The sun was front and centre in the clear, delphinium-blue sky and the air seemed to be scented with roses although she hadn't seen a single one.

It was as if the city were pulling out all the stops to prove it was worthy of the title of 'City of Romance'. It helped that currently it was host to the most beautiful man in the world, she thought, glancing sideways at Ettore.

He was dressed casually like a typical tourist in jeans and a T-shirt and trainers. Like every third man they walked past. But that was like saying a house cat was like a jaguar. There was something about how Ettore moved through the world, the way he carried himself, that made men straighten their backs and women glance over, then again over their shoulders as they passed by.

They were staying in an elegant hotel nestled discreetly off the Place de la Concorde. Le Grand Appartement penthouse suite was as grand as it sounded with velvet-covered sofas, antique furniture and a view across the city to the Eiffel Tower. The restaurant was close by, but equally discreet.

'Feeling restless yet?' Ettore leaned over and took a piece of asparagus off her plate.

She nudged her shoulder into his biceps. 'We only just got up.'

'It's our honeymoon, *dolcezza*. And we're in Paris. And I'm sharing a suite with the sexiest woman on earth.'

'So it's my fault you're acting like a silverback.'

He grinned. He seemed younger, freer than he had in Puglia. And he was young, she realised with a jolt. Too young to have had so much responsibility thrust on him out of the blue. Losing his brother, his mother, being injured himself and then having to step up and take care of the estate and his family.

How had he coped? He looked after everyone else but who looked after him now that his mother was gone?

'Are you happy?'

He looked stunned, as if nobody had asked him that question in a long time, then pleased. 'I don't think I've ever been happier.'

It was just words. It had to be, she thought. How could it be true? This wasn't real. It was a charade. Or that was how it had started. Now though this life with Ettore felt more real, more stable and constant than her so-called 'real life' had ever felt.

He leaned in, his mouth fitting to hers, and kissed her softly.

'What would you like to do now? I'm at your disposal.'

Her mind clicked through a series of X-rated images and his pupils dilated as if he were reading her thoughts.

She laughed. 'No, we can't. We're going to be civilised

and cultured. We're going to go up the Eiffel Tower and then I would like to go to the Jardin des Plantes. Would that work for you?'

He seemed stunned again as if nobody had asked him that question either. 'It would. It does. But I would also like to take you out to dinner.'

'Deal. Although, I don't know if Valentina packed anything that dressy.'

'That won't be a problem.'

It was a day she would never forget. Ettore was the best company, she decided. He was smart and knowledgeable, and she loved how curious he was about everything.

As they wandered hand in hand around the Jardin des Plantes, he asked her questions about the evolutionary diversity of plants and listened carefully to her answers. His golden gaze made her chest feel full, as though her ribs had shrunk. It wasn't an unpleasant feeling, just not one she could explain. Although she'd felt the same way back in Puglia when he'd told her that he would fly her home to England.

Home.

She tried to picture her small terraced house and her vegetable patch and her flowers. But it was like staring down through the ocean to the sea floor. She knew it was there, but it felt distant, blurred.

The Castiglione Fiana and its petal-strewn lawn was far clearer.

After visiting the gardens, they returned to the hotel and stripped each other naked, reaching for one another in the shower and then again in the bedroom.

'I suppose I should get dressed.' She stretched against

him, her back arching against his chest, her fingers curling into his hair, and he leaned over her face to kiss her.

'We don't have to—'

'We do. Everything else we did today was my choice. This is yours. And we don't have to stay for dessert.'

'You love desserts.' The smile that was breaking free on his mouth made everything inside her feel like warm honey straight from the comb.

'I do, but I love—'

Her heart was suddenly pounding in her chest because she was about to say *I love you more*. She felt dizzy all of a sudden. It couldn't be true. This was a deal brokered in anger in a hotel room in London. But none of that mattered now that she was here in a different hotel room in Paris. Because the truth was that she loved him.

And she wanted to tell him. Because he was the person she wanted to tell everything to. He was her everything. But the words stayed silent and unspoken in her head.

How could she tell him what she was feeling? This was a temporary arrangement. It didn't matter that they were having sex now or even that Ettore had brought her on this honeymoon.

Sex was intimate but it wasn't love. And just because her feelings had altered, didn't mean that Ettore's had or would.

'What do you love?' He was staring down at her, his light eyes intent, curious. A lock of dark hair had fallen across his forehead, and she smoothed it back, smiling.

'I love petits fours more. So, what shall I wear?'

'I'm sure Valentina packed something suitable. Go and check the dressing room.'

She slid off the bed and walked across the carpet, feeling his gaze follow her like a searchlight, liking the power her naked body had over him.

'I didn't ask her to pack anything special—'

She broke off mid-sentence as her eyes locked onto the dress that was hanging face-on from a hook on the door.

'Is that mine?' she said slowly.

Ettore was behind her, and she felt her body flutter to life as he leaned in to kiss her shoulder. 'It's not really my colour. So, I suppose it must be yours.'

It was a beautiful dress. The other dresses, the ones the stylist had chosen, were lovely but in an objective way. But this was a different kind of dress. 'Did you choose this?'

He nodded. 'I saw it today when we were in the car coming from the airport. I know you're not a dress person, but I couldn't imagine anyone else wearing it but you.'

'I love it,' she whispered. Her heart felt as if it were going to burst. 'It's beautiful.'

'I'll let you get ready.'

The dress fitted perfectly. She stared at herself in the mirror, pleased for once with her reflection. The dress was sleeveless, and the pleated silk was the colour of a robin's egg and the intricate ruffles on the bodice of the dress made her think of water moving.

When Ettore saw her, she felt naked again. His eyes burned into hers and as his gaze moved over her hungrily, it was like tiny flames licking over her body.

'Do you like it?'

He nodded. 'You look beautiful.' His voice was rough, his bedroom voice, and it was all too easy to imagine his hands on her belly and hips and between her thighs.

'You kept your hair loose.'

She nodded. 'Do you mind?'

'I like it. I like all of it.'

She liked the way he looked too in his dark suit and a crisp white shirt that he'd left loose at the neck. Nobody wore a suit like Ettore, she thought. He was just so intensely male and impossibly handsome.

Abruptly he leaned forward and lifted her face to his and kissed her hard until she thought she might melt into a liquid pool of desire.

'You're making it very hard for me to go out tonight,' he grumbled as he broke the kiss.

'Then stop kissing me,' she said softly. 'Come on, I want to make every woman in Paris jealous.'

Table Margaux was an astonishing restaurant. It was full but there was no sense of urgency. The service was low-key but efficient and the decor was *fin de siècle*, all eau de Nil paintwork and gilt mirrors and yet it didn't feel like a pastiche. As for the food.

'That was incredible,' she said as she put down her spoon and pushed her plate away.

'Would you like coffee or a tisane? Nightcap?'

She shook her head. 'Could we go back to the hotel?'

'You read my mind,' Ettore said, doing one of those minuscule uptilts of his head that managed to be both gracious and authoritative. *'L'addition, s'il vous plaît?'* he murmured as the maître d' appeared by the table.

As they walked into the private lift to their suite, their security detail melted away. 'Do they bother you?' Ettore glanced down at her. 'I can tell them to back up a little for the rest of our stay.'

'It's fine. I just forget about them when we're home.'

Home. That word again.

She felt Ettore's gaze pick over her profile and she wondered if he had picked up on it too, and, if so, what was he thinking?

'Speaking of home,' he said as they walked into the huge living area. 'I was wondering how you would feel about sitting in on a conversation I want to have with Gianni. About the estate? I have some ideas I'd like to run past him, and I could use your expertise.'

'You're pretty expert yourself.'

He smiled but it didn't reach his eyes. But why? Did he not see what an incredible job he had done at the estate?

'Barely. And I've made a lot of mistakes.' He gave her a smile. Or at least his lips curved into the shape of a smile. But his body told a different story.

'Shall we sit outside?' He gestured towards their private terrace, and she followed him into the warm, still air. Across the city, the Eiffel Tower was shimmering with lights, but she was too distracted by the strange, taut set to his mouth to do more than glance at it.

'Did you ever talk to him about it?'

'Who?' He stared at her blankly.

'Your brother, Edo. Before he died. About running the estate.' She was floundering suddenly. Ettore looked confused, but surely Edo was running it before Ettore. 'Or had your father not stepped down?'

'My father never stepped up.' He gave her a small, tight smile. 'Gianni's father, Stefano, oversaw the vineyard, and my father chased unsuitable women. When the bank got involved, I took over.'

'When was that?'

'I'd just started my final year at university. I had to drop out. But I was studying history so my degree wouldn't have been of much use to me even if I had graduated.'

Dulcie frowned. But that would mean…

'So, you were running the estate when we got married.'

'Yes. No. Sort of. Edo had decided he wanted to take over the running of the estate, so I took a few weeks off. To be honest, I was relieved. I was supposed to be this custodian, safekeeping everything for future generations, only I didn't know what I was doing, and then I met you, and it felt like everything was falling into place. I could walk away. Live the life I wanted. With you.' He leaned forward and rested his arms against the balustrade.

'But then we split up, and Edo was killed, and I had no choice. I had to go back.'

Dulcie frowned. No choice? Had to?

As if sensing her confusion, Ettore met her gaze, his forehead creasing. 'I love the castle. I love the history of it, and that it's a living, breathing, working estate. And I love my family, but I never wanted to be the heir. I was never meant to be.'

'So why did you stay? Why not let Stefano keep running it?'

'I couldn't leave. Not after Edo died.'

She remembered Ettore's face when Edoardo had given her the bracelet. 'You went back for your mother. She needed you.'

Ettore leaned more heavily against the balustrade, his gaze fixed on the lights fanning out from the centre of the city, his heart thudding against his ribs.

Below him, Paris stretched out into the distance. It

had been here so long, surely there was nothing it hadn't seen or heard.

'My mother thought I had died. When she realised it was Edo, she told me that the wrong son had been taken.'

Finally, he had said it out loud. And it felt so momentous that he half expected the lights to snap off or cracks to appear beneath his feet. But instead, everything stayed as it was. Except that Dulcie's hand was now wrapped around his. He felt her fingers tighten.

CHAPTER NINE

DULCIE FELT HER heart thud painfully as she replayed each of his words.

'I don't understand.'

She glanced over to where Ettore was staring across the city as if the breathtaking tapestry of light and shadow might somehow be able to help her make sense of his simple, devastating statement.

'It's not very complicated. My brother was her favourite,' he said, and the matter-of-fact tone of his voice was one of the most painful things she had ever heard. 'She adored him. He was everything to her.'

But even if that was true, she couldn't imagine anyone saying those words out loud.

'Maybe…' She faltered, not lost for words but robbed of them, brutally. Her own mother had been neglectful and erratic. She was also an addict, an alcoholic, so she said things that she regretted but nothing like that, and she'd loved both Dulcie and Oscar equally.

But Ettore's mother had been grieving, Dulcie told herself, trying somehow to rationalise the duchess's behaviour. She had been in pain, and shock, and she had been hurting.

'When did she say that to you?'

'She came to the hospital with my father.'

Her head was spinning. Did he mean after the accident? But Ettore was injured. He'd been concussed and broken his arm. She had seen the scars on his body from where he'd been dragged by the bike.

'They were away in Portofino visiting friends when the accident happened. Valentina called them but they were out for dinner, and it was noisy, and I suppose they got the wrong end of the stick. I was in bed when they arrived, doped up on painkillers but I don't think I'll ever forget her face when she saw me.'

He breathed out unsteadily. 'She looked devastated. And then she walked up to my bed, and she told me that I should have died, not Edo. She never spoke to me again.'

Dulcie felt sick, actually sick as if she might throw up.

'She was in shock. She didn't mean it.' She couldn't have meant it. It was so callous, so cruel.

'Sometimes I think that. But she loved him so much. And she didn't love me in the same way.' The bruise in his voice made her breath feel jagged in her throat. 'She blamed me for what happened. And I was to blame.'

His hands tightened around the balustrade, the knuckles whitening. 'It was my job to take care of him. To make sure he was safe.'

'But he was older than you.'

Ettore was shaking his head. 'I was always the sensible one. Edo was reckless. It wasn't just the gambling. He took risks. And he liked winning. I knew that. And I knew we were both wound up that night.'

'By what?'

'We'd argued. It didn't happen often. Usually, I backed down, but Edo had asked me for some money. Quite a lot of money and I said no. And he lost his shit. He just kept shouting at me and getting in my face and then he got tearful. He did that, when he couldn't get his own way. He had this whole routine. Shouting, crying, and if that didn't work, he'd call my mother.'

But Edo was in his thirties. 'Why would he do that?'

'Because he knew that she'd overrule me. That she'd take his side. Which she did. And then he was all smiles. He'd forgotten all about the race. And then out of the blue he told me he didn't want to run the estate any more. That he'd changed his mind. Just like that.'

Dulcie blinked as he snapped his fingers. 'He could do that. It was so easy for him. He didn't think about what it would mean. He just said it in this casual, offhand way. And I was so pissed off. That's when I reminded him about the race.'

He breathed in, a quick hard breath.

'We hadn't raced in years. When we were younger, it was something we used to do with our cousins. We'd race between the rows of vines on the dirt bikes. But then Stefano caught us, and he locked the bikes in the barn.'

'But Edo wanted to race that night.'

Dulcie phrased it as a statement not a question and he nodded. 'I don't know why. It was like he wanted us to be kids again. He was messing around, trying to make me laugh. Only then we argued, and he won, of course, and then he said that thing about stepping down.'

He looked suddenly exhausted. 'That's why I got on the bike. I knew Edo wouldn't be able to resist.'

His voice was barely a whisper now. 'And then he had to go and cheat. I was putting my helmet on, and I handed him his, and he rode off without taking it. You know, I don't think I've ever wanted anything as much as I wanted to beat him in that moment. To be number one.' There was so much pain and shame in his voice now that it hurt to listen.

'I could have just walked away. I should have let it go. Let him win. But I didn't. I chased after him. Even though I knew he wasn't wearing a helmet.'

'If you were riding different bikes, how did you both end up having an accident?'

'There was a gap in one of the rows. He crossed in front of my bike. His wheel hit mine and the bike flipped, and he got thrown off into the trees.' His words sounded slurred as if his mouth wasn't working properly.

'I remember my bike falling sideways, and my arm got caught in something and that's when it got broken and then I must have banged my head. Gianni found us. He called the ambulance. When I woke up in hospital, Edo was dead.'

Dulcie's heart seemed to hollow out inside her chest, and as she wrapped her arms around him, he leaned into her, his body shuddering.

'If I hadn't lost my temper, he'd still be alive. So you see, my mother was right. I am to blame. I killed my brother.'

'No!'

She spoke so emphatically that his chin jerked up.

'That's not true. It was an accident. And yes, Edo died. But you could have been killed too.'

'I should have stopped the bike.'

'What you need to stop is blaming yourself for what happened. Remember what you said to me when I said it was my fault that Oscar was like he is? You said that I can't change who he is on my own. That he has to take responsibility for himself. If that's true for Oscar, then it was true for Edo, too.

'He'll never change now,' he said quietly.

'I know.' She hugged him tighter. 'But whatever your mother said, that isn't your fault.'

'You know, sometimes I hated him. And Sofia too. I was so angry with them for being loved so unconditionally. But now I think that Edo felt trapped. I know Sofia does. We all felt trapped in different ways. But I couldn't see that then. All I could think about was how what I wanted didn't matter to Edo. To my mother. To anyone. I didn't matter. I never have. I'm just there to make things run smoothly.'

'You do matter. They all turn to you because you're strong and smart and because they trust you to do the right thing.'

She could feel his heartbeat slamming into her ribs. 'But I didn't do the right thing with you. I forced you to make an inhumane choice.'

She thought about her own father, callously discarding his son. Maybe he had reasons too. A childhood wound that had never healed. A wound that caused him to lash out, to hurt, to damage his own children. And she and Oscar were both in their own ways damaged. Like their mother, Oscar used drugs and alcohol to blunt his shame and pain. And she had this persona, an avatar she projected full of smiles and sunshine and peace on earth as if she were a Miss World contestant. But inside, she was just a little girl trying not to get hurt.

And Ettore was the same. More importantly he was

different from her father because he had apologised, and he was trying to atone.

'What about your father? Was Edo his favourite?'

Now he shook his head. 'No, my sister is his favourite. Probably because they're peas in a pod. She's pretty and flirty and completely irresponsible. She's never had a job. She's travelling, which basically means she just drifts from country to country, spending her inheritance and trading off the title she allegedly gave up. But if she calls my father, his face lights up like that tower.'

His eyes flickered towards the illuminated landmark.

Dulcie felt her chest tighten, and then she understood what had happened two years ago in London. And why it had happened. 'That's why you asked me to choose between you and Oscar, wasn't it?' she said gently.

The expression of sadness and shame on his face made her feel momentarily unhinged with a sadness of her own.

He didn't reply, but after a few seconds he reached up and loosened her arms, taking her hands in his and after another few seconds she realised that he was looking at their wedding bands.

'It sounds stupid, but I hadn't thought about your family. I knew you had a brother, but you didn't talk about him, so I thought you weren't close. Only then he turned up and you were so distracted, so focused on him. I could feel you shutting me out, and I panicked. I tried telling myself that you weren't the same as my family. But the more I thought about it, the more that seemed to be the point. You can't choose your family. You just get what you're given.'

His mouth twisted. It was the smallest thing and yet it wrenched at her heart.

'But you do choose your partner, and I didn't want to be with someone who was going to put someone else first. I couldn't be. I couldn't choose to live like that.'

'And I couldn't not choose Oscar. Not after my dad…'

'I know that now, but I didn't then.'

She closed her eyes, replaying that argument in her head, seeing Ettore's face hardening in the fading London light. She had thought he was being controlling, like her father. That she would not just lose Oscar, again, but lose herself. Become someone who had to curb her thoughts and feelings and dreams.

Staring into his eyes, she had watched the high walls go up but only seen them as barriers to block her out. She hadn't seen them for what they really were. Hadn't realised that Ettore was protecting himself from further pain, even though she was doing exactly the same thing.

'I made such a mess of everything.'

'No.' Now it was his turn to sound insistent and unshakeable. 'Look at me, *dolcezza*.' He slid his hands into her hair and tilted her face up to his and reluctantly she met his gaze. 'We both made a mess of everything. But the most important word in that sentence is not mess, but "we".'

Her heart was beating wildly. 'But this isn't real.'

'Isn't it?' His voice was soft, his caress softer still as he stroked her cheek. 'We're here in Paris, just the two of us. Right now, this feels more real than anything. And yes, we messed things up and we walked away from the mess me made. But we aren't meant to be apart, Dulcie. That's why we found each other again. And it'll work this time, I promise, because we've held nothing back. There're no barriers between us now.

His words made a bubble of happiness rise up inside her.

She leaned into his hand like a cat, then turned it so that she could kiss his palm. Gently she twisted the ring on his finger.

'You matter to me. You always mattered to me. Even when I hated you for breaking my heart. You know, all the girls at my school used to talk about "the one". This mythical man you would see across a crowded room and boom. That would be it. And because I'm a scientist, I just thought, yeah right. That's never going to happen to me. Only then I saw you at the airport and I thought it was the storm making me shake. But it was you. You made me shake inside.'

'When I saw you, I couldn't breathe. I thought I was having a heart attack. You were holding a teddy bear, and you were turning round as if you were looking for someone.'

She frowned. 'I forgot about the teddy. It was lying on the pavement when I got out of the taxi. Someone must have dropped it by mistake.'

Ettore was shaking his head. 'I was so scared that your husband was somewhere with the baby, and you were trying to spot them in the crowd.'

'No baby. No husband.' Her fingers splayed out over his wrists, and she felt his pulse twitch. 'I wasn't looking for anyone. Not then, not ever. Not until I saw you, and then I couldn't look away.'

His eyes were all pupils as he leaned in, tracing the shape of her lips with his tongue.

'Sweet,' he murmured. 'My sweet Dulcie.'

His words vibrated softly against her mouth and something liquid pooled inside her body as he reached up to touch her throat, fitting his thumb into the hollow at the base. He sucked in a breath, lifted the heavy mass of her hair from her neck and sucked the spot where her pulse was hammering against the delicate skin, as if he were savouring her hunger.

She moaned softly. Heat was drifting up over her face and she felt unanchored with need for him.

'Ettore…'

She pulled him closer, lost in the hungry press of his mouth and the fluttering waves of pleasure spilling over her skin.

'Put your hands on me, here.'

She was grabbing for them, but he was already cupping her breasts, trapping the pebble-hard nipples between the middle and index fingers in a way that had her arching forward.

He groaned against her mouth, and she was pulling his shirt free, her shaking fingers tugging at the waistband.

'Not here.' She reached for him, but he was shaking his head, laughing softly. 'Not here, *dolcezza*.'

With shock, she remembered that they were still outside on the terrace.

He lifted her up, and she curled her legs around his waist, and he carried her back into the bedroom. And then he was pushing the fabric of her dress down from her breasts, and she took a strangled breath as he sucked her nipple into his mouth, his stubble scraping against her skin.

'I want to undress you,' he said hoarsely.

She shivered, the directness of his words sending a flickering electric current over her skin. 'I want that too.'

Heart shuddering, she watched him peel the bodice

away from her body, down over her stomach, and then he slid his hands under her bottom, and she felt the warm silk flutter over her thighs.

Stepping back, he stripped off his clothes and then he was naked too, standing there in the softly lit room, his powerful, beautifully muscled body gleaming like bronze, his cock jutting away from his groin.

She stared up at him, her mouth drying. She felt as though she were made of need, and yet she still needed more.

As if he could read her mind, he leaned forward, his mouth finding hers, and he kissed her hungrily and then he slid his thigh between hers, and she felt the jab of his cock against her belly as he nudged her backwards until she half fell, half sat on the bed.

'*Cosa vuoi che faccia?* Tell me what you want. Tell me what you like.'

'I like this.' Her fingers wrapped around his cock.

He grunted, and she gasped as it swelled to fill her hand.

'Not as much as I like it,' he said as she pushed him back against the mattress. It felt great. But it would taste better and, leaning forward, she shifted her fingers to the base of his cock and licked up the shaft, swirling her tongue over the straining head, up and down, her own hand moving to slide between her thighs.

She moaned softly, because that felt good too, and then Ettore was pulling her back.

'It's my turn to taste you,' he said hoarsely.

He shifted his weight, moving down the bed, and her nipples tightened painfully as he pressed the flat of his palm between her legs and she tried to push back against his hand, only it didn't happen because Ettore pulled it away but then he lowered his mouth and she felt his tongue dip into the slick, quivering heat like a hummingbird.

She moaned then, and she didn't know exactly when, but her hand had moved to clutch his hair. Pleasure was flooding through her like a smooth, fast-flowing river. The water was roaring in her ears. Or maybe it was her blood. It kept flowing faster and faster, only now it was undulating too, the swirling currents growing stronger and stronger and faster and stronger…

'Ettore…' She moaned out his name, the last syllable hovering in the air.

Her fingers clenched into a fist, pulling his hair tight, and then her spine arched, muscles spasming, as the currents pulled her under and she clung to him because she would drown if she let go.

After what felt like a hundred years but was probably only sixty seconds, Ettore lifted his mouth and moved up her body, and she reached for his cock, guiding him inside her, relishing her power over him as his face creased with the effort of holding back.

He was rock-hard, bigger than he had ever been, and his breath was shallow as he pushed in deeper, stretching her, lifting her higher, pressing her closer.

'Cazzo.' He groaned, his eyes glassy, the skin across his cheeks drawn. 'I'm going to—'

She felt his hand slide down to cup her bottom, and she wrapped her legs around his hips, and a thick, stifled groan erupted from his mouth like the noise an animal might make as he buried his head against her throat. She felt his body tense and he jerked back in a way that nearly pulled them apart and then he was surging inside her, clutching her against him as she clutched him.

They stayed like that for longer than her brain could keep track of. An hour, three? It didn't matter. And all that mattered was that this was real. Not just the sex, but what she was feeling. What he was feeling, she thought as he tightened his arms around her and kissed her over and over, his chest rising and falling in time to her heartbeat.

She couldn't be imagining this, not now. Not with his body so heavy on hers that it was impossible to tell where he ended and she began.

She wasn't imagining it. The next morning, they woke late and made love until they were exhausted.

Or rather she was exhausted. Ettore had astonishing stamina, Dulcie thought as she watched him swim laps in the suite's private rooftop pool, feeling drowsy and warm in the Parisian sunshine.

But it was the right kind of drowsiness. Not that fatigue that made her feel as if she were wearing one of those weighted vests but the good kind that was accompanied by an absence of her usual racing thoughts.

She felt calm and clear-headed and alive. *You could just say happy,* she told herself. Because she was happy.

It was something she couldn't remember feeling for a long time either. But everything she needed and wanted in her life was here. Her chest tightened. Except her brother. But, fingers crossed, Oscar would reach this same place of calm and certainty one day.

'Stop it,' Ettore said softly, dropping down beside her on the sunlounger, his face serious.

'Stop what?' Raising her hand to block the sun, she

squinted up at him, feeling more than a little envious of the droplets of water that were trickling over his glorious body.

He ran his hand back over his scalp, smoothing the hair. 'Feeling guilty about Oscar.'

'I wasn't,' she protested. 'Well, maybe I was a little,' she confessed as his eyes found hers.

'We can bring him to Paris when he leaves the clinic if you want.'

'We could?'

Her voice was high with surprise, and he reached over and tilted up her chin so that their eyes were level. 'Of course. He's your brother. I want you to spend time with him. I want to get to know him.'

'And I can't wait for Oscar to get to know you too. I want him to know what a lovely man you are.' She clasped his face with her hands and pressed a clumsy kiss to his mouth. As they broke apart, he shifted his weight forward to pick up a croissant. He held it out to her.

'You should eat. We've got a busy day.'

'Have you got something planned?' she asked as she dipped her croissant in her coffee.

He nodded.

'I thought we might head out to Giverny.'

'Really?' She dropped her croissant in her coffee. 'I've always wanted to go there.'

'I know.' She felt her heart flutter as Ettore fished the pastry out and swapped his cup for hers. 'You mentioned it yesterday when we were at the botanical gardens.'

Only in passing, but he had noticed.

'Have you been before?' As he shook his head, she

felt suddenly, stupidly elated. It was new to them both. They could discover it together.

The gardens were every bit as stunning as she had hoped. There was an artistry and an exuberance to the planting that just blew her away. The closest she got to artistry was doodling in her notebook. But she could see how using plants with delicate, fluttering flowerheads such as gypsophila and bee blossom could recreate the shimmer that was so characteristic of Impressionist art.

'This is what I want my garden to look like,' she said as they crossed a wisteria-clad bridge over the water-lily-strewn ponds. 'Unfortunately, I don't have the space for a pond.'

'You do now,' he said softly.

'So I can let my imagination run riot back at the castle,' she teased.

'Wherever, whenever you want.'

They ate lunch at a small bistro in the village, which had no menu but was clearly a favourite with the locals. Unsurprisingly, given that the food was simple and fresh and perfectly seasoned.

In the car on the way back to Paris, she checked her phone and there was a photo of Oscar wearing shorts and a T-shirt. He looked flushed and sweaty, but triumphant and the photo was captioned:

Couch to 5k. First run. To be continued...

'That's fantastic,' Ettore said when she showed him the photo. He kissed her softly on the mouth. 'Trust the process. He'll get there.'

'Did you check your messages?'

He nodded. 'Just the usual. My uncle wants to talk about an investment opportunity, which is almost certainly code for some debt he's amassed. And Gianni has a couple of things he wants to discuss but they aren't urgent. Oh, and Carlo called.'

'Who's Carlo?'

'My lawyer. He sent me a note offering his congratulations, but I'm guessing he wants to update my affairs to reflect the marriage.'

'You mean a post-nup.'

'Yes, but a post-nup isn't just for me. Of course it will protect the estate. But it's for you, too. To make sure you're protected. And I want to protect you, Dulcie. You and Oscar.'

She bit her lip. 'I don't want to make any kind of claim on the estate. I know you probably think I do because I took your money.'

'You borrowed the money. And you've already paid back the first instalment. How did you do that, by the way?' he asked as the car stopped smoothly.

As they walked into the hotel, her mouth twisted into a shape that made the air in his lungs bunch in his throat. 'I had some money I put aside for emergencies. You know, for when things get out of hand. But hopefully, there won't be as many of those after Oscar gets out of rehab.'

'You don't need to rely on hope any more,' he said gently. He hated the idea of Dulcie living in a state of high alert and, reaching out, he took her hands in his. 'And if, if there's an emergency, you have four hands now instead of two.'

She nodded slowly, and some of the tension left her

face. 'Thank you. And I am going to pay you back in full. I just need to get a job. I don't want to be like your uncle or your cousins.'

'You're not like them.'

'I'm going to prove that to you.'

'You already have… What?' His forehead creased as the lift door opened. 'Why are you smiling?' He let her into their suite.

'It's just us talking about the hard stuff like it's easy.'

He stroked her face. 'You make it easy.' Their eyes met, and he felt the blue of her irises deep inside like a fork of lightning and a shiver of heat scampered over his skin.

Cazzo.

He swore silently, shoulders tightening as his phone juddered across the coffee table, and he had to force himself to glance down at the screen. No, he thought, not now.

'Aren't you going to answer it?'

'It can wait. It's just Carlo.'

'It's fine.' She smiled, a sweet smile that he wanted to capture in a jar. 'I thought we could order room service for dinner. I'll go get the menu while you talk to him. Do you know what you want?'

'You choose for me.'

He leaned in and kissed her softly on the lips and then his face altered fractionally, his voice too as he answered the phone, his gaze following Dulcie as she walked back into the living room.

'Ciao, Carlo. Come stai? Sì, sto bene.' He laid the phone down on the sofa, tapping the speaker icon so that the conversation would be audible to Dulcie when she joined him. He would introduce her to Carlo when she returned and, in preparation, he switched to English. Carlo

worked with a lot of international clients, so he was fluent in several languages.

'Thank you for your note. It was very kind of you and Carolina.'

'My pleasure. I know you said you were taking a few days in Paris and as a friend I want you to enjoy your mini-moon, I believe it's called. But as your lawyer, and given that you've been married for two years, it's my professional duty to ensure all aspects of your financial and legal well-being are secure. As you know, marriage legally creates a binding contract with rights and responsibilities. Financially, it can affect taxes, inheritance, and it can lead to shared assets and liabilities.'

'I know, and I apologise for the subterfuge of my actions. Dulcie and I met and married very quickly and when we separated we were both in shock. But neither of us wanted to end things permanently. We just had to find a way back to one another.'

Glancing up, he saw that Dulcie had returned and was leaning against the door frame, the menu in her hand, her eyes soft on his face.

Carlo laughed. 'Well, love works in mysterious ways. But again, as your lawyer I have to say that your marriage is excellent news. Now that you've fulfilled the Corti-Marchesi clause in the will, I can see no further impediment to your inheritance of the estate and the title.'

Ettore felt his body stiffen. Even without looking in her direction, he could feel the impact of the lawyer's words on his wife.

'I need to go, Carlo.'

'Of course, of course. Let me know when you're back and congratulations again.'

As the lawyer hung up, Ettore switched off his phone and got to his feet.

'Dulcie—'

'What was he talking about?' The stiffness in her body had edged into her voice. 'What's the Corti-Marchesi clause?'

'It doesn't matter.'

He started to walk towards her, but she held up her hand. 'It sounded like it did. It sounded like it mattered a lot. I mean, fulfilling it means you inherit everything, right?'

Her face was blank of expression, but he could see the shock, the wound in her eyes.

'Yes, it does, but—'

'And to fulfil it, you had to get married?'

'I have to be married before the current heir's death.'

'Must have been annoying when we split up, then. I guess you must have thought you could find a replacement pretty quick.'

'I didn't think that. I didn't even know about the clause until three weeks ago.'

'And then you came to find me.'

She blinked as if she were trying to wake up from a dream. 'You said you wanted to make your father happy and then you offered me money to help my brother. You made me feel as though you were doing me a favour but all the time you were looking after yourself.'

'Not myself. The estate, the castle. You've met my family; they would wipe out six hundred years of history and the livelihoods of an entire community in a matter of weeks if one of them inherited. I can't let that happen, *dolcezza.*' He took a step towards her, wanting to take the pain from her eyes.

'Don't call me that.' Her voice was cold like ice, but fragile too. And he knew if he took another step forward it would crack.

'You expect me to believe that you care about those people? You didn't want the responsibility. You told me you were going to walk away. Or was that a lie too?'

'No, I was planning on leaving. Before I met you, when I pictured my family, I never saw myself. Fiana was the hardest place in the world for me to be happy. But then you came to Puglia, and it was the easiest.'

'And you expect me to believe that.'

'It's the truth.'

'Like it was true when you told me we needed to stay married because you wanted to make your father happy.'

'That was true. It still is—'

'And yet you didn't tell me about the marriage clause, did you? Even though that was true too.' Her mouth pulled into a smile that was utterly and heartbreakingly sad. 'For the same reason you didn't tell me you were a marquis. You didn't trust me.'

'I didn't know you like I know you now.'

'And I didn't know you. I still don't.' Her fingertips were white where they were biting into the door frame.

'Yesterday, you said we could make it work, make us work because we'd held nothing back. But you were lying—'

'I wasn't. I'd forgotten about the clause because it didn't matter to me any more. Look, when I came to Cambridge to find you, I was going to tell you that I wanted a divorce. Then I saw you and I knew that I didn't want to let you go. I didn't want to lose you, again. And I knew that Oscar needed help, and you needed money to help him, so I offered to pay for his treatment.'

'You wanted a divorce?' She was staring at him as if he were a stranger, and then she was moving past him into the dressing room.

'What are you doing?' Heart pounding, he followed her in. She was shutting the safe. Her hands were shaking.

'Here. Take this.' She grabbed his hand, yanking open his fingers, and he looked down, his lungs seizing.

She had given him her wedding ring.

'You wanted a divorce. You can have one.'

'I don't want that. I want you. I love you.'

'You don't know what love is. You used me. You manipulated me. Just like my father did. You twisted the facts to suit your agenda. Never mind about Oscar. You let me believe I was doing a good thing, that I was bringing comfort to a dying man. But all this time, it was about a castle? About money? Don't you dare tell me that's love.'

'I have to, because it's true.'

She snatched up her bag, her face pale and taut. 'Love. Lies. Truth. Nothing you say means anything. Here. This is yours too.' Her fingers fumbled with the clasp of the bracelet and then she tossed it to him.

'My father gave it to you.'

'Because you lied to him.'

'Dulcie, wait.' He made to grab her arm, but she was running now, out of the door and into the corridor.

She cannoned into a trolley laden with towels and cleaning products and then she was running again.

'Sorry.' Ettore righted the trolley for the startled-looking maid, but when he got to the end of the corridor, Dulcie had already disappeared.

CHAPTER TEN

'A PINT OF FERRYMAN'S, a rum and Coke and a couple of packets of cheese and onion crisps, please, love. Can you put it on my tab? The name's Anderson.'

'Of course.'

Smiling, Dulcie selected a pint glass and angled it at forty-five degrees directly under the tap, straightening the glass as she poured.

This was her second shift at the Crown and Gown, and she was still checking off the steps of pint-pouring as she went. But there was something calming in the process, and she felt a small uptick of satisfaction as the beer separated to form a creamy head.

Right now, she would take her wins where she could.

It had taken almost six hours to get back to England from Paris. Somehow, she'd managed to flag down a taxi to take her to the airport, but even the thought of walking into Charles de Gaulle had made her want to burst into tears and she'd made the driver turn around and return to the city.

She must have looked pretty unhinged, clutching her passport like an amulet because the driver had suggested she take a train instead, and he had dropped her at Gare du Nord.

There were no tickets for the first train leaving so she had to wait for the next one and that hour seemed like the longest of her life, and she couldn't relax or even sit down until she was safely on the train and the sprawl of Paris was replaced by countryside.

It was too late to get a train back to Cambridge. Instead she booked into a hotel near St Pancras. She was so strung out and emotional she thought she would never sleep but when she curled up on the bed, her eyes shut and she woke up nine hours later, still fully clothed with the familiar, pale London light flooding the room.

She stayed there for two more nights, buying food and eating it in the room, watching the city wake and then return to darkness. She slept a lot, mainly because sleep anaesthetised the pain. But each time she woke, Ettore was the first thing she thought about.

And it hurt. Everything ached and she understood then why Oscar drank and took drugs. But it was thinking about Oscar that pulled her back from the cliff-edge. Because he needed her, and she needed him.

She needed Ettore too, and she missed him like an amputated limb. Missed him so much that it was easier just to stay another night. But when dawn rose again, she checked out. In that liminal space between Puglia and Cambridge, she could slow time, pretend to herself that she was travelling but never actually reaching her destination, like Sofia or Holly Golightly. Because then she would have to admit that it was over with Ettore.

But they were done. She knew that now.

And she had done enough pretending.

It was time to start living for real. To make some changes, because she wasn't the same woman now.

She glanced around the pub. Most people were enjoying their drinks and the sunshine in the garden that stretched back to the Cam, the river that meandered through the city and had given it its name. The pub itself was cool and quiet, in contrast to the inside of her head.

But some of that noise was starting, finally, to fade a little.

And with each tiny, baby step she took back into the world, it faded incrementally.

The first step was putting the house on the market. If she was going to put the past in her rear-view mirror once and for all, she needed to pay Ettore back. It wasn't just that she didn't want to be beholden to him.

There couldn't be that connection between them even if it was just a three-digit amount next to the word 'monthly' and Ettore's name.

It was his name that was the problem. Seeing it written down, saying it inside her head, was enough to make her spiral.

To make her yearn.

To make her hope.

In short, to do what she'd done in the hotel off St Pancras.

She needed to move forward.

Before the agents had put up the For Sale sign, the house was under offer. The buyers had no chain and were desperate for the house, the agent said. More importantly, they were cash buyers.

So, this morning she had gone to the bank and asked for a bridging loan to tide her over until the sale went through. The bank had agreed, and twenty minutes ago she'd sent the balance of what she owed to Ettore and closed her standing order.

And now she had done it, she felt so many differing and conflicted emotions. Relief. Pride. Astonishment. And sadness, because selling the house hadn't just broken the connection with Ettore. It was her last link with her dad. He had given her the deposit for her original flat in London before he'd severed all ties with her.

Strangely, splitting up with Ettore had given her closure with her father. For so long, she had feared him, then she had hated him. But now she knew that he must have acted how he had because he was damaged. She would never know what or more likely who had inflicted the harm, but it made it easier to forgive him.

As for her mum, she had forgiven her a long time ago.

The house was still hers but she had decided to move out so she was renting a room from one of the professors at the college. She would sort out something more permanent in a couple of weeks. But for now, she liked the smallness of her situation. She felt like a snail, carrying everything she needed on her back. She had just one bill to pay, one bedroom and a bathroom to keep clean and tidy. It meant she had less to think about.

More time to think about the big picture. And the big picture was taking shape. Incredibly, she had come up with a business plan for working with country estates to bio-diversify their lands. She had even come up with a name: The Green Canvas Collective.

It would start small but if she had even a tenth of her dad's brain for business and her mum's energy, it would work. That was part of the bigger picture too: remembering her mother from before she became ill. They were snapshots. But she knew they were true because they chimed with the way Oscar was now.

He was still in the clinic. But she could see the progress he was making in the photos he sent and hear it in his voice when they spoke. There were setbacks, but he was inching towards that calmness and certainty she had longed for in Paris.

Paris.

Ettore.

It was only a sliver of time since she'd last seen his face or touched his skin or felt her body soften beneath his steady gold gaze, and yet it felt like a lifetime.

It felt like yesterday. Would the pain ever disappear completely? She was shocked by how much it hurt. More so even than the first time because a part of her had never quite let go of him then. Now, though, she knew they were over.

She had left him high and dry.

Not quite. Despite what she'd said in Paris, she hadn't told her solicitor to get in touch with Carlo Biondi for the very good reason that she didn't have one.

Whether Ettore was her husband or not, he was the best man to run the estate. To oversee the vineyard and the charitable trusts.

She pictured him on the floor at the *casa-famiglia* playing that game with the teenager in the hoodie. In another life, in another country, that boy was Oscar. What would happen to him if Ettore was forced to step down and hand the reins over to Checco?

It would be a disaster. Everything would fall apart. The money would evaporate, and people would get hurt, damaged children like Oscar.

But married was still married even if you were separated. And she would stay married until Ettore inherited the estate.

And then she would divorce him, or he could divorce her. Her ego could survive either. Her pride demanded that she prioritise the lives of people who had done nothing to deserve the consequences of her and Ettore's actions above her personal pain and the need for absolute closure.

She pressed her hand against her chest.

The pain changed on an hourly basis. Sometimes it was sharp like now when she was stupid enough to think about Ettore. But even when she was busy or distracted, the pain remained. A constant, dull ache, and with it a longing, a yearning for him that was so persistent and ridiculous that sometimes she would start laughing.

Only then she wasn't laughing, she was crying.

But he was gone. Just like those hailstones in Paris. Her dreams of love had melted away, but she would not let it define her life or her brother's.

If she told herself that often enough, surely it would come true. Wouldn't it?

As the car pulled slowly to a halt, Ettore stared up at the familiar crenellated outline of the Castiglione Fiana. He had half considered staying on in Paris indefinitely. But he couldn't keep hiding from the truth for ever. Couldn't hide the truth from his family for ever either.

And now he was here, he felt something like relief.

But then, things had changed. He had changed.

Dulcie had changed him. Throughout his childhood, his parents' open favouritism for his siblings had left him feeling rootless and superfluous in his own family. He had made himself useful, leaning into his natural affinity for order amid chaos.

But it had stifled him. His life had narrowed in ways he didn't want but felt powerless to change. Because his value, his only value to his family, lay in what he could do for them, not in who he was or wanted to be.

And then there was Dulcie with her blue, dancing eyes and her sweet smiles and her courage and he'd been forced to face their past. To see that he had put conditions on their love in the same way his family made their love conditional. Acknowledging that had given him the courage to change his life.

To put down the survivors' guilt that he'd carried since his brother's death.

To grieve for Edo and know that his grief wasn't tainted somehow.

Dulcie's words had been a restorative balm to his mother's angry outburst. She had been like a nurse plant brought in to care for the vines.

It was why he saw the estate differently too now. For the first time in what felt like a very long time, he didn't see thc raw-edged, big-skied land that had belonged in his family for centuries as a burden to be carried or a privilege that required a drip-feed of sacrifice.

Now it was his living and his home, and he had fallen in love with it all over again.

As he had fallen in love with Dulcie all over again.

And her reward?

He had lied to her. He had told her that there were no secrets between them. But there were. And when she'd found out the truth, he had lost her.

And now he was losing his mind.

After Dulcie fled the hotel, he waited in Paris. Hoping, praying she would return. Leaving the hotel at dawn, he retraced his steps through the city, even returning to the hotel they had stayed in when they first met.

And then Valentina called him and said that his father had been taken ill and was asking for him and he had a choice that was not a choice. Just like the one he had forced Dulcie to make when Oscar turned up in London two years ago.

His chest ached for the pain he had caused her. And then his pain had intensified two hours ago when he'd realised that Dulcie had paid back every penny she owed him and, finally, he was forced to accept that she had fled to England. And that for the second time in his life, their marriage was over.

'Ettore.'

His father was sitting up in bed with an oxygen tank on the floor beside him. He looked pale and small and relieved. Not at all like his father.

'Papà.'

Leaning in, he kissed his father's papery cheek. 'How are you feeling? Valentina said you were struggling to breathe. She had to call the doctor.'

'I'm fine.' His father waved his hand dismissively.

'Is that what the doctor said?'

'Oh, I only let him come and see me to keep Valentina from calling an ambulance and the fire brigade. Sit, sit.' He patted the bed. 'It's ghoulish. Keep calling the doctor every two minutes. I sent him away. Dying men should be left to die with dignity. Or better still a magnum of champagne.'

'You're not dying right now, Papà. And sending the doctor away is not helpful.'

'And you want to help me, do you?'

He felt suddenly exhausted. 'Of course I do. Is this about Sofia?' Obviously, it was. It was only ever about Sofia.

But Edoardo shook his head. 'It's about you. My son and heir.'

There was something in his father's voice that made his body tense.

His father shifted on the bed. 'Everyone thought your brother was like me. It's flattering for a father to be told that. But Edo was the spit of your uncle. Your mother's younger brother, Marco. That's why your mother doted on him. Spoiled him. And he was easy to spoil. Like your sister. Like all of your family, me included. We're party-starters, lotus-eaters. But you, you were always different.'

Ettore stared down at his father. Where was the old man going with this?

As if to answer that unspoken question, Edoardo gestured towards a portrait of a dark-haired man with clean features and an intense, fulminating gaze.

'You're like my grandfather. Piero Ettore. He wasn't set to inherit the title but, as you know, his brother drowned when his yacht capsized, and your great-grandfather stepped up. What you might not know is that he saved our family from financial collapse. My father, of course, carried on the more typical family tradition of embezzling and bed-hopping behind closed doors. It is his mess that you only recently managed to clean up.'

Ettore shrugged. 'It's what I do.' He'd done it so many times in his life, he should be an expert, and yet here he was, newly estranged from his wife for the second time. If that wasn't a mess, he didn't know what was.

His father's eyes were fixed on his, and for once they weren't languid or mocking.

'And you do it very well.' Edoardo took a gulp of oxygen and breathed out shakily.

'Too well, I think. It confines you. And I'm sorry for that. But I'm extraordinarily grateful and pleased that you are my son and my heir. Edo, I think, would have struggled, and failed.'

He took another gulp of oxygen.

'And I think he knew that. It made him angry and reckless.'

Edoardo closed his hand over Ettore's wrist.

'I loved your brother. I miss him every day. I know you do too. But you were not to blame for his death. Your mother was upset, horribly upset, but she was wrong to say what she did. I was wrong not to make that clear before now. I was wrong not to protect you from her grief.'

Ettore could feel his father's pulse beating through his skin.

'Why now, Papà? Why are you telling me this?'

'Because the truth hurts, but sometimes it's better to face it than hide from it. Because you are here, and Dulcie is not. And the two of you have been inseparable like a pair of heavenly twins.'

There was a gentleness to his father's voice that he had rarely heard. The last time, in fact, had been when he gave Dulcie the bracelet.

He pulled it out and it sat glittering on the palm of his hand.

'Dulcie isn't here because we broke up. In Paris.'

'I know.'

His father smiled. 'Your wife wrote me a letter. A note, really. But she made good use of every word. Very eloquent for a scientist. It caught me off guard. Made me think about things I should have said or done. Regret a few things too. But that's what old men do, isn't it?'

Ettore stared at his father mutely, his blood thin and airless. In the dizzying panic of the morning and his misery and the rush of questions and conjectures Edoardo's confession might have prompted, only one mattered. 'Dulcie wrote to you.'

Nodding, Edoardo reached over and picked the book from his bedside table. He pulled out an envelope. 'Here, read it.'

Ettore opened the envelope and stared down at the handwritten note.

Dear Edoardo,
I wanted to thank you for being such a wonderful host during my time at your beautiful castle, but also to let you know that Ettore and I are not together any more. It hurts to write those words, but my pain is not your concern. Your son's is. Ettore loves his family so much. He would do and has done everything to keep you all safe and secure in your way of life. Please look after him and give him the love he deserves.
Dulcie

P.S. Don't be stubborn about ageing. Use your sticks and your oxygen because growing old is a gift. Embrace it. And embrace your son.

Ettore stared down at the sheet of paper, his heart a dead, lead weight against his ribs, Dulcie's words burning in his brain.

'She says that you're not together, and you aren't. But it still strikes me as odd.'

'Odd?'

'Apparently you would and have done everything to make sure your family is safe and yet, in the same letter, she's telling me to look after you and give you the love you deserve, which sounds to me as if she has and *would do* anything to ensure your happiness. So, on paper at least, you seem very well suited to one another.'

Ettore stared at his father. 'I don't know why she would write that.'

The old man shrugged. 'And you won't find out if you don't go and talk to her.'

'She doesn't want to talk to me. And she shouldn't. I lied to her, I manipulated her. I hurt her. I made a mess of everything.' His voice cracked and he pressed his hands against his temples as if doing so might crush the truth of that statement into dust.

'So go clear it up. That's what you do, isn't it? Clear up messes.'

'I let her go, Papà. I pushed her away twice. Twice. I mean, once is a mistake but twice is unforgivable.'

His father snorted.

'That sounds like something written on one of those appalling little magnets people stick on their fridges.' Edoardo sighed. 'I'm not good at love myself but I know it when I see it and you love Dulcie. And as a gambling man, and judging by the changes I saw in you when you brought her here, I'd lay odds that you never stopped loving her. Nor will you. And don't imagine for one moment that you'll get over her. Absence is cruel like that. Hence, my regrets.'

Reaching over, he patted his son's hand.

'But you're not an old man like me, Ettore. You don't need to spend your remaining days on earth marking time. You're young and smart and you have a life to live. Not here with me, but with Dulcie.

'And in case you've forgotten, you share a name not just with your great-grandfather but a great warrior. So go and fight for the woman who wrote me this letter. The woman who loves you. The woman you love. Because when two people love one another, truly love one another like the two of you, nothing can keep them apart.'

CHAPTER ELEVEN

THE BOTANICAL GARDENS in Cambridge were always quietest in the early afternoon. There was a distant hum of traffic and the nearer, insistent hum of the various insects and bees that were most active at this time of the day.

As usual the insects outnumbered the people, but that was fine by her, Dulcie thought, straightening up from the bed she'd been weeding.

She was in the Mediterranean section, which was hard. The scent of the plants and trees that were native to that region kept tugging her back to Puglia so that periodically she would unravel a little between the orchids and asphodels. But it was early days. By winter she might be cured.

Leaning forward, she deadheaded a plant that wasn't dead and was suddenly close to bursting into tears again.

'Dulcie!'

Breathing in sharply to stem the burning sensation in her eyes, she wiped her hands on her trousers and turned. Alison, the head gardener, was walking towards her, talking animatedly to the man walking beside her. No doubt, it was some random member of the public asking for horticultural advice.

No, it wasn't, Dulcie thought dully, a moment later.

She was rooted as firmly to the spot as the cedar tree

behind her, a drum roll of panic beating against her ribcage because, even at a distance and with the sun in her eyes, she recognised the man. And there was nothing random about his reappearance in her life. And she knew with certainty that many winters would pass before she would be cured of the pain he had caused her.

'There you are.' Alison beamed at her. She had a slightly dazed look on her face, and there was a flush on her cheeks. 'I know you're just finishing up, but this gentleman has a very interesting question about the role of mycorrhizal fungi, and I thought you would be the best person to talk to.'

Keeping her gaze fixed on the other woman, Dulcie smiled stiffly. 'I'm not sure I can help.'

As Ettore stepped forward, she had to press the soles of her shoes into the soft earth to stop herself from turning and running because being that close to him again, knowing that she would never get closer, was agony.

With a light stubble dusting his perfect jawline and his golden eyes narrowed against the sun's rays, he looked heartbreakingly beautiful but sombre in dark jeans and a grey T-shirt and for a moment she forgot the past and the pain. For a moment she just stood there, drinking him in, her body aching for his touch, and she wondered why that ache in her chest was worse now that he was within touching distance.

'Perhaps it would help if I got into the specifics.' Ettore's deep voice cut into her thoughts. 'What I'm particularly interested in is how they form symbiotic relationships with vine roots to enhance nutrient uptake. I understand you have some experience in that area.'

She felt Alison's gaze on her face. 'A little,' she admitted.

There was a buzzing sound that had nothing to do with the bees, and the head gardener frowned, patting the pockets of her trousers. 'Sorry, I have to take this.' She smiled at Ettore. 'Dulcie will take care of you.' Still smiling, she retreated and there was nothing to be done.

They were alone. Even the bees seemed to have drifted away, and Dulcie could hear the nearness of him beating in her blood.

She cleared her throat. 'What are you doing here?'

He met her gaze, and a cold shiver scraped down her spine, and yet it burned. 'I find being outside calms me.'

Her pulse stumbled. 'I meant in England. In Cambridge.' Her face tensed and she covered her mouth with her hands. 'It is Edoardo. Is he—?'

Ettore took a step forward, his forehead creasing. 'No, he's fine. Or he was when I spoke to him an hour ago when I landed.' His face tightened. 'I'm sorry, I didn't mean to scare you.'

'I thought something had happened to him.'

Her shock and panic had morphed into an anger that was audible in her voice and for a moment she thought it would spark a similar anger in Ettore. But he didn't react. Instead, he stared past her to a clump of pale pink asphodels. The same asphodels that grew in the gardens of his castle where he had kissed her to the point of helpless oblivion.

'Something did happen,' he said finally, and her heart thudded as his eyes found hers, his gaze reaching into her, holding her still.

'To be more accurate it was someone, not something.

You happened to him. You wrote my father a letter and because of that letter he and I had a conversation about the past and Edo and my mother. And it helped. It helped me, a lot.'

She breathed in sharply. 'I'm glad.' And she was. Even though it had ended between them, she wanted him to be happy.

'I'm glad too.' His eyes were hard and intense, and there was a tension in his spine as if he was fighting to stay in control.

'But not as glad as I am to see you,' he said then, and maybe it was the simplicity of his words or the softness in his voice but the tears she had been holding back filled her throat and she stumbled backwards, holding up her hand.

'No. You can't do this again. I can't do this again. I've changed, and besides we said everything there was to say in Paris.'

He held up his hands like a soldier signalling his desire not to fight.

'I know we talked in Paris, and everything you said then was true. I lied to you. I let you think that my only reason for wanting to stay married to you was to comfort my father.'

His face stiffened, and he breathed out shakily.

'But I also lied to myself. Because I wasn't there for my father. I wasn't there for the castle or the title or the money. I was there for you.'

Gazing down into Dulcie's small, still face, Ettore felt breathless with the utter relief of seeing her again, and finally telling her the truth, and nothing but the truth.

He was still wearing the same clothes he'd worn as he

walked into Edoardo's bedroom, because after speaking to his father, he had got back in the SUV and been driven straight back to the private airfield and flown to a different private airfield near Cambridge. And then another car had driven him to the botanical gardens, and he had collared the first person he saw who appeared to be working there.

It had all been so easy up until that point.

This was proving harder. But he was here to fight for Dulcie. To fight for their future.

'I could have got my lawyers to contact you. But I came to England, to Cambridge, because it was always about you,' he repeated slowly. 'The chance to see you, to be with you again. And that's why I'm here now. Everything else I can live without, but I can't live without you. I didn't make that clear in Paris.'

Dulcie was staring at him, her blue eyes wide.

'What are you saying? That you're going to give up your job and your castle and your jet and your aristocratic lifestyle to move to England?'

He nodded. 'Yes.'

She took a step towards him and even though her face was flushed and there was a smudge of pollen on her cheek, he thought she had never looked more beautiful.

'You can't do that. You need to run the estate.'

'I can do it, and I will. I've spoken to my father. Gianni is a very capable manager.'

'But he's not you. You understand the finances. You have vision and imagination. And you care about the estate in a different way because it belongs to your family, and it's your home.'

'Not without you. It's just a building and some fields.'

He shifted slightly to give her space, not crowding her, not pushing her to make a choice, because she wasn't the only one who had changed.

'You hurt me.'

'I know.' His voice shook slightly as he met her eyes. 'And I wish I could turn back time and be the man you deserved, the man you needed…'

'You are the man I need. You always were. There's never been anyone for me except you. Even when I hated you, I loved you.'

His heart twisted with hope.

'I couldn't forget you because I never stopped loving you,' he admitted. 'That's why I couldn't let go. Only I couldn't admit that to you. Not then. I was too proud. Too stupid. Too cowardly.'

'You're not any of those things.'

'Do you believe that? Is that why you wrote to my father?'

As she nodded, her hand found his. 'I couldn't let go either.'

His fingers tightened in hers and Ettore pulled her against him, breathing through the tears clogging his throat.

Dulcie buried her face against his neck, breathing his scent, her heart beating steadily now.

'Are you staying in London?'

'I'm not staying anywhere.'

'Then where's your luggage?'

Ettore frowned. 'I don't have any.'

Dulcie laughed. 'Are you joking?'

'No, I didn't pack anything. After I talked to Papà, I got on the jet and flew here. It's okay, I lent this beautiful blonde some money and she paid me back today. She puts money aside for emergencies and I guess getting rid of me was an emergency.'

His eyes found hers. 'I know losing her felt like one.'

'I sold the house. I'm renting a room from one of the college professors.' She leaned into him. 'I can't believe you came all this way to talk to me.'

'Not to talk to you. To fight for you. To fight for us.'

Dulcie stared into his beautiful light eyes, seeing the softness there and the heat. Her hands gripped his T-shirt, squeezing the fabric in her fists.

'I want that too. But we can't fight here. The gardens shut soon. But maybe you could come home with me.'

'Is there room?'

'There's plenty of room. It's a castle.'

Ettore stared down at her in confusion, his eyes searching hers, and she loved him then for his openness and his need and his courage and because he was hers.

'You said it wasn't a home without me. But what if I was there?'

They stared at one another steadily, each allowing the possibility that after so many missteps they were finally in the right place to make their marriage work.

'Then I would be the happiest man alive.'

'Then we match. Because I'm the happiest woman alive,' Dulcie said huskily and Ettore lifted his hands and cupped her face and kissed her, his arms tightening around her as the bees started to hum again.

EPILOGUE

Five years later...

'MARELLA KEEPS ON winning. It's not fair.'

Gazing down at his son's tear-streaked face, Ettore felt his heart contract, remembering all the times he and Edo had raced one another. He still thought about his brother most days but no longer with the guilt he had carried for so long.

Dealing with the memories of his mother was still a work in progress but, as with Edo, he found that they were more varied and less damning than he had once imagined. And his past, the bad and, increasingly, the good, acted as a guide rail for his own parenting.

Because he was not just a son and a brother now, but a father too.

He made his voice serious, giving Giovanni's question the consideration it deserved. 'Your sister is faster than you, but she has longer legs because she is four and you're two.'

'I'm nearly three,' his son said quickly. He loved his sister, but it didn't stop him railing against the unfairness of her being two years older than him. And a faster swimmer.

Ettore smiled. 'Yes, you are. And one day your legs will be as long as Marella's because her legs aren't going to keep growing, are they?'

Giovanni thought for a moment and then shook his head. 'But I wish I was bigger now.'

Ettore leaned forward on the sunlounger and took his son's hands. 'I know, but you make bigger splashes than Marella when you kick.'

'Only a little bit.' Marella was standing next to her brother now, her blonde hair a mass of damp, unruly curls. 'But you are two years younger than me so even a little bit is a lot,' she added begrudgingly.

'That's true.' Ettore took his daughter's hand and pulled her in for a shoulder bump and she gave him a heart-melting smile that she had inherited straight from her mother along with her blonde hair and her love of nature.

'When's Mamma going to be here?'

'Any minute. She's just having a nap. Why don't you practise being floating stars while you wait for her to come down?'

'And then can we have ice cream?' Giovanni said, his light brown eyes widening hopefully, his tears forgotten.

He nodded. 'You can.'

'Come on, Gio.' Marella took her brother's hand and then she turned and kissed Ettore on the cheek. *'Ti voglio bene, Papà.'*

'And I love you both too. And no running.'

Heart swelling with love and pride, he watched them walk back to the pool, their little legs stiff with the effort of not running, Marella's hand clasped tightly round her younger brother's.

Officially, it was a working day, but he had already prepared for tomorrow's meeting with the Ministry of Agricultural, Food and Forestry Policies. Today he could afford simply to enjoy life with his family.

A lot had changed in the five years since he and Dulcie had got back together. They had renewed their marriage vows and had two children. And three of their wines had been awarded Tre Bicchieri by the prestigious Gambero Rosso guide.

But the greatest changes had happened with his family. He had called Sofia after he and Dulcie had returned from Cambridge. They had talked about the past, but mostly about the present and, to his surprise, Fia had asked to move back into the castle. More surprisingly she was a doting aunt.

As for his cousins. They were still unpredictable and wayward but the changes he'd made to his own life had rippled through the entire extended family. His door was always open, but he had made it clear that there would be no more handouts. No freeloading. Everyone had to earn a living.

And in another surprising development, Checco had stepped up and proved himself a capable team player.

Ettore glanced over to where Edoardo was dozing in the sunlight. But it was the change in his relationship with his father that mattered the most. Because against all the odds, Edoardo was not just alive, he was thriving. Incredibly he was following some of his doctor's orders and every day he made it clear that Ettore was the son he didn't just tolerate but loved.

And he loved his grandchildren too. Equally.

Ettore felt his spine stiffen. His skin was prickling

and even without hearing the children's shrieks of excitement he knew his wife had just walked onto the terrace by the pool. Inside, outside, in a crowded room or in the darkness, it made no difference, he always knew where she was.

Knew too, and this gave him as great a pleasure as his children, that she was where she wanted to be. With him, here at Castiglione Fiana.

Now, he turned his head and allowed himself a moment of pure, indulgent pleasure to watch Dulcie walk towards him while everything else stilled and softened into silence.

Dulcie.

His beautiful wife.

His soulmate.

The sweetness in his life.

His gaze moved in silent appreciation over her bikini-clad body, and he felt a rush of heat tighten his muscles, some very specific muscles. It was their seventh wedding anniversary today and they had celebrated in the dawn light, reaching for each other wordlessly, their need as raw as it was when they first met in Paris.

They had exchanged gifts. From Dulcie, a letter written by his namesake and great-grandfather, which she'd had framed. His eyes fixed on his wife. Dulcie was wearing his gift. A sapphire and diamond necklace to match the bracelet his father had given her all those years ago.

She still looked like that woman who'd rolled in with the storm in Paris trailing thunderbolts and hail in her wake. Her blonde hair was longer now and lighter from the Puglian sun and there was a smattering of freckles on her shoulders that he liked to join up with his tongue.

'Ciao.' She leaned in and kissed him softly on the mouth. 'You let me go back to sleep.'

She turned and waved to the children in the pool.

'You were up a lot in the night. I thought you needed to catch up.' His hand moved to touch the curve of her stomach, fingers caressing the smooth, taut skin as if he were testing it for ripeness. 'This one's got quite the kick. I don't remember Marella or Gio being quite so rowdy.'

She shook her head. 'I know. Good job you ordered those hail nets. We might need them to stop this little force of nature from causing havoc once he or she is born.'

He leaned in to kiss her stomach. 'On the advice of my very clever wife.'

Dulcie felt her heart flip over as he pulled her onto his lap, his mouth seeking hers, and she kissed him back greedily. It didn't matter that, only an hour ago, she had tasted him and teased him and made him groan out her name as her thighs clenched around his hard, proud body.

'My very sexy, clever wife,' he murmured against her throat.

'You have a one-track mind.'

'Not true.' His hand moved over the curve of her hip. 'I have a whole bunch of delightfully scenic routes to take me where I want to go.'

She laughed and then he was laughing too, because more than anything he loved to see her happy and she was profusely, blissfully, rampantly happy, living here with Ettore, building a world of their own.

A world that was welcoming and inclusive. It wasn't just Fia who was living with them now. A year after he finally left rehab, Oscar moved to Italy. He didn't live in the castle. His choice. He had wanted, needed, his independence. But he also needed his family close by so Ettore had arranged for a cottage on the estate to be renovated.

And Oscar was happy too. During his stay at the clinic, he had discovered a talent for pottery and now created beautiful pistachio-green *schizzato* bowls and jugs and platters in his studio. But it was his relationship with Ettore that gave her the most happiness. True to his word, Ettore was a strong and stable presence in her brother's life and the two men were close friends now.

Of course, there were bumps in the road, diversions and potholes, because life was complicated. But they knew how to deal with them now. And they wanted to deal with them. Because they loved each other for better, for worse.

'So you're still travelling?' she teased.

He shook his head. 'No, you're stuck with me, *dolcezza*.'

'Says the man trapped under me.' She leaned in and kissed him fiercely. 'But just so we're clear, I'm not stuck. I chose you.'

'So no itch, then? I mean, that's what happens after seven years, isn't it?'

'To other people. Not to us. We can't be separated. We're *vite maritata*.'

'Always.'

His gold eyes gleamed in the sunlight and her throat thickened with love and happiness as Ettore pulled her closer and kissed her with the same fierce tenderness as she had kissed him.

* * * * *

Were you blown away by
Marchesi's Marriage Mandate*?*
Then why not explore these other
passionate stories by Louise Fuller?

Boss's Plus-One Demand
Nine-Month Contract
Royal Ring of Revenge
Business Between Enemies
Billion-Dollar Baby Clause

Available now!